NATHAN UNWRAPPED

Susan Saxx

www.BOROUGHSPUBLISHINGGROUP.com

NATHAN UNWRAPPED
Copyright © 2020 Susan Saxx

ISBN 978-1-951055- 91-2

To all those who have so kindly and lovingly cheered me on and supported me - my wonderful family, dear friends, my two amazing feline bosses and my incredibly supportive beta-readers, without each and every one of you none of these stories would be possible.

I appreciate and prize you all. I'm the lucky one.

ACKNOWLEDGMENTS

No book gets written without lots of support, and I'm grateful to have had it.

A big thank you to all my writer friends who have supported me through the years and been there so generously to brainstorm, chat, beta-read, and struggle with me through all the various revisions of my books.

A singular, unique acknowledgment to one special lady: Dayna. Your skill and smarts, patience, and above all kindness and heart have impacted my work and personal life, so much. Thank you for being so smart and savvy…and for letting me be a part of your life.

A special thanks to Alexia R. and Michelle P, two of my closest companions in crime, for their ongoing encouragement and very real support. I love you both.

Last but not least, a humble thank you to my publisher for taking a chance on me.

NATHAN UNWRAPPED

Prologue

Nathan

Nathan stared at the mess in the musty old room.

Rows of artist's canvases rested against the walls, paint-spattered drop cloths tossed over them. Broken-down easels sat stark in the faint glow of light from the tiny window. Piles of dust, half an inch thick, clung to everything. Everything that had once been a central part of his life.

He shuddered. Time had stretched way too long since these items had been used. Touched. Savored.

Loved.

His heart panged like a fresh jolt of pain into an injured limb. Just like… No, he wouldn't say it. Think it. He was on his own now. Solo. He would stay that way until he drew his last breath.

But the words still forced themselves into his consciousness. He'd tried to rip them out of his mind time and again. But they persisted. Raw, accusatory. Judgmental and truthful.

These forgotten canvases were like him. Their time, their relevance, over and finished. His gaze flicked over the paintings. Silent and lifeless slices of his past, they were discards from a museum no one ever visited or even knew about.

Once, these canvases held all his hopes. Like brilliant orbs of fire, building in him, blinding in their intensity, they'd had to emerge. The realization that the crazy images that poured out of him, the unusual compositions that scared even him at times, were actually good had come as a shock. Then, the subsequent knowledge that he could actually take concepts that were deep, full of pain and worry, and yes, sometimes even hopeful, and transfer them to the canvas… It had opened his dark life up to a brief era of goodness.

But now, all the things that had once carried such hope were voiceless. Dead.

Like every other thing that had ever started to grow in him, these too remained frozen in time, in eternal stasis.

The room swirled in front of him until he was back to *that* day.

The sunlight poured through the tiny window, him stripped to the waist, painting like a wild man, the sound of the Atlantic crashing on the beach in the tiny cove of Refuge Bay in the background. Exuberant. So many ideas flowing from him, there simply wasn't enough time. Composing, creating, connected to something far greater than him. Crazy in his creations, but underneath it all he was joyful. Until....

He stepped back abruptly, jarred out of the memory. He reached down, not knowing what drove him, and yanked off a drop-cloth that was tucked carefully around one canvas. Clouds of stagnant dust exploded in the air. He quickly took in the painting, and remembered. It was the one he'd been working on when... There it was. He winced as he saw it, even while knowing full well it would be there. Hell, he'd dreamt of it often enough.

A gaping black hole, bottom right, desecrating the painting. Another massive rip tearing down from the top to that ungodly intrusion.

Pressure built in his chest. He'd worked so hard to come back to this, to set his eyes on everything once again. But now the plan was in front of him, now the mission—the sole thing that had kept him going all this time—was within reach, and he was actually here.

Could he make beauty out of this travesty, out of the pain that threatened to swallow him whole? Could he bring it all back to life once more?

He stumbled backward and almost fell over the box of tools he'd brought with him. He scrambled to stay upright. The room started spinning. He'd been a man who had looked every challenge in the eye then faced it down and conquered it with the spirit of a warrior.

Now, he turned away and ran.

Chapter One

Nathan

"You think you bought enough animal cookies?"

Nathan scanned the six boxes scattered on the floor of the old farm kitchen amidst all the unpacking, and turned a cold eye on Zach, his best friend since the year he'd flunked kindergarten. "Can there *ever* be enough animal cookies?'

The tea towel Zach flung at him caught him by surprise and, as luck would have it, around the throat. As Zach had been using it to wipe down the ever-present dust on the old, faded red kitchen counters, it wasn't the best companion piece for his worn t-shirt. He grabbed the towel and tossed it into the empty box that held the stinky, day-old garbage.

He peered down his shirt, attempted to brush off the tiny gray mark of clingy dust that had already caught, and gave Zach hell. "Hey. I actually washed this last night in the bathroom sink, then hung it to dry. Don't be fucking it up."

"*Sorry*, your highness. I forgot you're trying to look well-organized and in control. Might I add, that's a losing proposition? Both the look *and* the condition."

Nathan grabbed another cardboard box from the haphazard tower in the corner of the large kitchen, set it on a beaten-up wooden chair, then grabbed his utility knife and scored a quick line in the packing tape.

Crazy Zach and his mind games.

But crazy or not, Nathan would never trade his friend for another. Zach had stood by Nathan's side through everything, always loyal, always there. They had never been romantically entangled. Romantic love came and went, but a real friend was gold.

He peeled back the cardboard wings. "And why would that be?" He tossed him a quick look. "By the way, I'm praying you don't answer. I'm not in the mood for a lecture."

Zach snorted, tossing the ingredients for a poor man's omelet into a chipped ceramic bowl. "Whenever your prayers hit higher than the ceiling, we'll all be in trouble." Zach's gaze landed on the old, puke-green, overstuffed chair in the dining alcove. He scooped up the open box on it and angled it toward Nathan.

Another five boxes of animal cookies. Or six.

Nathan groaned. So much for careful planning. His mind had been in such a flurry when the old house had suddenly come on the market. There'd been so many details to take care of and this time, they all mattered. The down payment, the offer. Especially with the state of his finances.

He'd withdrawn from life the last five years, and that didn't pay well.

But this was important. Manor House *had* to stay in the family. It had been with the Gentaels for five generations, maybe more. He couldn't bear to lose a family legacy, or the history that came with the house. Tall and stalwart, with the gorgeous time-weathered, golden-hued brick, and endless nooks and crannies inside, all of it filled with memories.

As a kid, he'd spent summers on the peninsula. The lush tip of land speared into Refuge Bay, which opened into Chesapeake Bay and out to the deep blue Atlantic. Life had been simple here, but rich. Oh, so rich.

His family had been sheltered, as had so many others.

He'd had hope here in the midst of all the confusion. He'd been embraced by the community and at one with the vibrant nature all around him. The gulls and sandpipers, the pale yellow starfish, even the hellbenders. And, of course, the sea. The stunning, changeable sea he could see from the property, hear the waves crashing.

Especially since his horrific stint in the military, saving this house meant more than ever. He couldn't see it go. The last shred of the life he'd known, extinct. Then everything really would've been lost. With all the things he'd already suffered, it would have been too much.

So, he'd bought the house. Barely.

And now its survival, and the survival of the plans for his life's mission, all depended on someone else. Again. More specifically, on currying the favor of the last investor on the long list they'd started out with, and snagging him hard.

Nathan's gaze flickered to the scarred leather portfolio tucked behind the boxes in the front hallway. All the names, all the men he needed to track down when all this was done. He'd peeked into it last night when he was looking for the strength to continue, to keep cleaning this old place when he was so bloody tired.

His dream was to have Manor House filled once again. This time with those who needed her. A few acquaintances from college came to mind, though, more than for any others, it was for the guys he'd served with. Some of them needed this place badly. The peace here on Refuge Bay. This old, quiet, cautious house that sheltered everyone within its walls, while she gave them the refuge they needed to get strong. Be strong.

She was going to recall them to life.

"Why so many sweets?" Zach's comment yanked Nathan back from his musings.

He searched quickly for a good reason for the excess stock. "Well, you love them, right? You know there are storms out here on the peninsula. In fact, Jonesy next door told me earlier that his bones say we're getting one today. A doozie, he says. So...."

"There's no storm in the forecast. I know, I checked. Clear and blue. Gorgeous spring day."

"But they *do* come, and when they do, it's fast. Supplies don't get through. The peninsula gets cut off from the mainland, and that can go on for days. So, when this one hits, we'll have—"

"Yeah, yeah." Zach grinned. "You should have used that brilliant mind of yours to be a storyteller, not an artist. Or an animal cookie thief. You're amazing in those areas."

Nathan could tell when he'd lost a battle, and besides, Zach knew him through and through. "Shut up and put on some coffee." He grabbed a box of cookies. "We'll polish off this one right now."

Zach plunked a big box down beside the Mason jars on the big wooden kitchen table, grabbed the old dinged-up metal coffeepot they had to boil water, held it under the spout, and when nothing came out, smacked the tap hard on the side.

Reverberating screeching echoed through the kitchen along with an intense vibration on one whole side of the house. After long moments the water sputtered then streamed out.

"Voila." Zach's brows rose as Nathan stared at him. "Hey. All it needed was a little love."

Nathan snorted. "I've heard the noises of your kind of love through too many walls, and in college, through a sheet." He shook his head. "Start brewing."

"Yeah, yeah." Zach nodded, dug around in another box, and pulled out the French press. He filled the well-used gold sleeve, gave a dramatic wince at the bargain brand coffee, then grabbed a couple of paper plates out of the cupboard. "I'm not hungry, but you need to eat. How late were you up?'

Nathan dropped onto the patchy linoleum floor. The huge, scratched-up red and vanilla tiled squares were, without a doubt, almost dizzying. He sighed. At least he'd swept and scrubbed all of these damn squares this morning. It had taken two full hours, and that included the hardwood floors in the hallway and the rest of the first level.

One huge task off the *getting ready fast* list. The sooner he got it prepared for that last New York investor to go through the place and fork over the money, was the moment Nathan could start breathing easy again.

Until that happened, his insides remained cramped. He'd be up late every night. He'd slept when his body gave out.

He hadn't finished airing out the damp basement, a mess left over from one of the earlier floods, the last time Refuge Bay had been cut off from the mainland. The big fans he'd carted in hadn't quite done their work yet. It would all have to be attended to once he got the money.

Thank goodness he'd had a head start before the guy from New York showed up. The rest of the potential investors had had a million excuses why the place wasn't worth their time or money.

This guy was Nathan's last hope. Thankfully, their real estate agent had been willing to share the man's contact information. "It's a long shot," she'd said. "Guy's hard-nosed, ex-military, but he's got cash. He's administering his family's charitable trust, and he's got to get that settled fast. If you get in with him...." That hard-nose was due in two days.

Enough time to get the place in shape, while hiding most of the major flaws.

This wasn't how he normally operated. He'd always been aboveboard, squeaky clean. He'd played straight and honest all his life, yet when he'd done things by the book, the people he loved most had been hurt.

He'd gotten the message, he thought as he grabbed the subpar milk from the fridge, determined to keep going on endless coffees. Time to do what worked. He'd be damned if he'd let anything get in the way.

He was a new man now. Maybe not a better man, quite possibly a much worse one, but one who was going to get things done.

Chapter Two

Nathan

Zach poured the steaming coffee into big, mismatched mugs.

"Ahh, smells heavenly. Thanks."

"I'll put another pot on. So, how late, exactly, were you up?"

"Not that late," Nathan fibbed. He grabbed a magic marker and started outlining a humorous caricature of Zach on the side of one of the cardboard boxes. *Just to keep in practice.* A few deft strokes and he appeared. He'd start working on one of the house next. "And hey. I appreciate you getting me up this morning. I really didn't want to sleep in when there's all this to do."

Zach shook his head at the cartoon, biting back a grin, then narrowed his gaze as he refilled the pot. "'Not that late.' You think I'm stupid? You've got to start taking care of yourself."

Nathan sighed. "Sorry. I know. But Sal said everything's got to be perfect for this guy. He's fastidious to the max. But once we get him hooked, I promise, I'll take a long nap." He caught Zach's look of concern mixed with a glare. "A *really* long nap."

His friend looked like he wanted to say something, then pressed his lips together.

Protecting me again. For a guy who'd sworn off any and all serious relationships, Zach sure took care of those he loved.

What a damn waste.

He reminded himself he was in the same category. He'd sworn off all relationships, but for an entirely different reason.

Zach handed him his mug, then dropped onto the floor across from him and settled his back against the end cupboard. He turned his head, taking a long look around the ancient kitchen they'd spent so much time in when they were younger. "Place has great bones, you know. I've always loved it. Even though it's a holy mess right now."

"Well, at least I got the damn floor done." Nathan breathed deep, felt his body fight between the ever-present tension and letting go and relaxing.

Zach leaned back and sipped the hot liquid, eyes closed. "A perfect country morning. It's so peaceful here, despite the stuff Livy said about being worried about a burglar."

Nate knew he was referring to their conversation with one of the neighbors up the lane.

"Well, let's make sure we keep an eye out. I don't want any surprises. Not now." He exhaled a long breath. "Especially not when—"

Suddenly, a huge noise burst into the room, and the back door shook hard, slamming in the frame.

Zach jumped, gasping, "What the *hell*?"

But Nathan was already up, adrenaline shooting through him.

Bracketing the door into the wooden frame on both sides with his hands, he peered out the curtain-laden window at the top of it. He gazed down, and he couldn't turn the doorknob fast enough. The door shot inward as a big, full-body mop of white, tan, and black straggly fur heaved itself through the opening, leapt and planted its paws on his pecs, propelled him backward, and slammed him against the wall.

"Molly. Girl, I missed you."

Whining and intense doggy yips emitted from the bundle as the animal went crazy. Nathan hugged the gyrating beast, and was rewarded with a wet tongue anointing his face.

He hugged her, and memories of summers here on the bay flashed through his mind. When he was a teenager, Molly was nothing but a pup, following him everywhere. Down to the beach. Into the forest, when he'd been scared, taking along his sketchbook to get to the clearing where it was magic, having the courage because of Molly.

Zach was hovering. "*The* Molly? She's still around?"

Nathan could barely tear himself away from the dog, and satisfied himself with grabbing her scruffy white face, holding it between his two hands, and planting a big kiss on her forehead. He nodded at Zach as she squirmed in his grasp. "The Molly."

Zach smiled, then wrinkled his nose. "Nate, she's amazing, but she's wet, dirty, and stinks like—"

Suddenly, a jet-engine-type roar came from outside. Nathan grabbed Molly's collar to steady her as she jerked him. Zach jolted too, then pivoted toward the old dirt driveway that rounded the back of the property. A sporty car was sitting there, still running. Some guy—*built*—was standing looking at his phone.

"Holy shit," Zach muttered.

"What?"

Molly yanked free, tore through the kitchen, mud flying and splattering everywhere. She rounded the old wooden table, the one they'd been unpacking that held Nathan's gram's box of jarred preserves.

Molly continued her mad dash and took out the southeastern corner of the table. The shaky old leg on that side buckled, and the massive table top tilted. Six fat jars of Gram's cherry preserves did a crazy slow-motion dance, slid to the edge of the pock-marked table—and off.

Cherries flew everywhere. Nathan glanced and, oh yeah, there was even one up on the wall above the silly retro black cat clock. His t-shirt would never be white ever again.

Zach spun toward Nathan. "The *special* jars?"

Nathan nodded as the strong smell of alcohol permeated the air. Gram's good old-fashioned, special emergency recipe. Preserves done in one hundred proof rum.

And Molly wasn't done.

She galloped, slamming into a tower of boxes. When that tumbled, a clang of pots and pans and the sack of quinoa that apparently had a leak in a box came to life. Then she took off for the living room.

Nathan yelled, "Stay." She didn't.

The rumbling outside the door stopped abruptly. Nathan glared at Zach. "Who the hell is that?"

"I don't know. The license plate is…." Zach's voice trailed off.

Nathan stopped in mid-bound toward the living room. "What?"

"Nate. The plate's from New York. It's the guy from New York."

Chapter Three

Og

The place was a dump.

There were telltale signs of water damage around the foundation. On an addition on the side of the house were obvious signs of patchwork bricking done around most of the windows, and the chimney.

The house was a lean, long sentinel in the midst of trees and overgrown bushes, out here on this godforsaken peninsula, where obviously nothing good ever grew.

But there *was* a freshness in the air, a nip of cool along with the undercurrents of a definite warmth ready to banish the last remnants of winter. He spied a little cottage too, run-down, a short distance from the house.

Og stepped from his beloved 1973 Mustang and shut the door. *Stella* always took care of him, and was one of the best females to have ever come into his life. He'd found her at a scrapyard years ago, and had restored her lovingly while he sorted out his personality—too brash—and his sexuality—not the one he'd expected. A few women had been pivotal in his life, but they'd mostly lost touch once he'd gotten back from Iraq and opened his gym, an homage to boxing.

Without boxing and the ability to legally pummel fellow humans into the ground, he doubted he'd have gotten through his reentrance into society without being arrested. He'd managed to stay out of the pen, and kept legal long enough to inherit what his great-grandfather had left him and his brother: a charitable trust.

Having all that bank tied up in a trust wouldn't have mattered, except for his brother Michael, who needed the cash desperately. Og didn't have it to give to him. The trust was tied up in a thousand legal knots. Og had to get creative.

He approached the house. Another ridiculous deal, yet another way to make the money he'd been given stewardship of work and grow. Og had found when he channeled his rage and angst into investing, he learned how to gobble up smaller companies, and do some import / export on the side, making the trust a fuckofalot of money.

Action was where it was at. Nothing happened without a strong plan, one that was implemented boldly, damn what others thought.

Og strode toward the house, taking in the surroundings, scrutinizing the roll of the Atlantic, and he had to admit, the view was stunning.

He'd left the city yesterday. Traffic and two major accidents had him stopping overnight in Wilmington, Delaware. He left before reveille would've sounded, and it still took him five hours to get to this godforsaken place.

Necessity being the mother of invention, Og had to look over this junker. He'd gotten the call from Palmer's assistant. Time was running out. The big man was losing patience. Find something by the end of the week, she'd said, or Og wouldn't be able to score with Palmer and get on full-time, and not only as a consultant. Og had to find a sweet deal, nail it, and make it pay off.

So, two damn long drives, and a hotel bed. Then, half an hour ago, he found himself fighting with the GPS, which didn't have all the country roads uploaded into it. He'd stopped up the lane when he couldn't find the way to the house, and a lively old woman with an English accent had given him the craziest instructions on how to get here. Some of the phrases had been "third flowerpot on the right," and "the birdhouse with the yellow paint on the rooftop," along with a warning to not leave his "fancy car" unattended if he didn't want anything stolen since there seemed to be a burglar in the area. Her favorite blanket had been taken right off the clothesline, and she'd pretty much detailed its history to him.

He'd shaken his head, thanked her, and took off. Her directions were bizarre, but incredibly precise. Now, he was here standing in the shadow of a chimney that had a cherub on top of it.

Time to do business.

He walked around to the front door when the smell of booze hit him like the inside of a brewery.

This should be interesting.

Chapter Four

Nathan

The drop in Nathan's gut was all too familiar. If the pushy investor came in now and saw the disorder, everything would be lost. The only thing he knew that could make his existence even remotely redeemable would all be gone. Again. He didn't know if he could recover from that kind of loss.

This was his last reboot. Absolutely the last.

Nathan ran to the back door, slammed it shut and turned the lock, then jumped to the kitchen window, hurriedly yanking the curtain closed.

"Dude. What are you doing?"

"Hiding."

Zach shook his head. "Buddy. He had to have seen the curtains open."

"*Pfft*. Guys don't look at curtains."

"But the noise. The commotion in here, and the alcohol stench…"

"That souped-up ride would've drowned out the waves on a Nor'easter." Nathan catapulted to the basement entrance, yanked out the extension cord connected to the fans downstairs, and tossed it down the wooden stairs. Then he hurriedly flipped the light in the corner off. "We'll be super quiet. Wait him out. He won't know any different."

Nathan slid down against the wall, tucked himself into the corner, looped his arm around Molly, who'd finally come back to his side, grinning her slobbery grin, and held her close. He motioned for Zach to join him.

None of this made sense. But hell. He was acting on instinct. "When he's gone, we'll contact the agent. Reschedule. Clean up. Then—"

Zach's expression said *you're crazy*. "Nate, he's not stupid. Even if he's an investor with way more money than those great big balls he's supposed to have, he'll know. You can't—"

A loud voice filled the air, coming from the far end of the kitchen by the hallway from a man in knife-edged khakis, a distressed brown leather jacket and matching brown leather boots who had wide shoulders and dark hair curling around the nape of his neck over an open-throated shirt. He was definitely not amused, and communicated it by aiming a blistering stare at Nathan and Zach.

Shit. The front door was propped open in the hope the breeze would get rid of the mustiness. Instead they got a pissed-off investor.

The man surveyed the shambles. Turned a withering gaze on the sloppy slosh of preserves, already leaking into the un-waxed tile floor. Noted the quinoa mountain, with bits tracked everywhere. He sniffed the air and shook his head.

He looked at Nathan and faced him with a *you better listen up now, peon* gaze.

"Always good to walk in on an in-depth discussion about my balls. Something I heartily endorse. They're really quite amazing. But most importantly, do they get a walk-on?"

Chapter Five

Og

"Molly, *stay*." The Adonis's arm tightened around the big dog's neck as he hugged her close and stared up at Og. "Did you happen to see that thing at the front of the house?"

"Thing?" Og asked. "What thing?"

"Big piece of wood. Got this round metal doodad halfway down. People press their finger or hit their knuckles against it. It's a custom here in the United States when people want to enter a dwelling not their own." His gaze raked Og and for a moment he felt like he was the one at fault. "When the people inside the dwelling want you to come in, they open that big piece of wood. If they don't, basically, it means fuck off. Voilà. Social contract. Everyone knows where they're welcome, and where they're not." He gave him a *got it?* look, then said, "Priceless."

Og stifled the urge to raise a brow, and instead flexed his shoulders and leaned lazily against the doorjamb. "Yeah, I've heard that shit." He stared into the man's eyes. Warm and brown. So inviting, you could dive into those depths.

But warm or not, no one was going to mess with Og's investments. "I've also heard the one where people who want somebody else's big buckets of cash tend to welcome them, and be really nice to the one *with* the big buckets of money. Because, as you know, if I want something, I should be nice to the one *with* the something. Basic common sense. Barter and trade. One of the first rules of getting to use something that's actually *not* yours. Heard that one?"

And dammit all if the Adonis—aw, hell he was more like a poet, with that wavy hair, the soft curls that brushed the collar of his shirt in the back—didn't blush. Og's breath caught a little.

Fascinating. The way the red crept up the man's face, and how the rest of him seemed so alive. On fire.

But Og was here for a business transaction. Nothing else.

And definitely not to break up what looked to be a happy couple.

The guy at the sink—not Adonis—slid his feet into a couple of thin flip-flops, picked his way through the shards of glass littering the floor, and came forward, hand extended. "I think we're getting off on the wrong foot. Sorry, but it's been a crazy morning, as you can see. I'm Zach Lees. This is my currently seriously sleep-deprived friend, Nathan Gentael, who's been cleaning all hours of the morning until our friendly neighborhood Big Foot came by. I take it you're the investor Sally Gardin set up the appointment with? Ryder? Rydel?"

Ah. The bodyguard.

Okay. He could play this game. "Jake Reiden." He grasped Zach's hand, shook it. "Call me Og."

Surprise crossed Zach's face, but he hid it quickly. "You'll have to pardon Molly over there. If there's anything going on, she's got to be part of it, which often causes," he threw out his arm, "mayhem."

And true to his word, the canine was writhing and whining even louder, trying to break free from Nathan's hold, straining toward Og. Even that was a nice picture. Sensitive dude, communing with nature. A bit arousing.

"Nate, I think you better put her outside because of all the...." Zach's gaze skirted the ring of broken glass around them and he winced. His gaze moved to the dustpan and broom in the corner, a distance away.

Hell. The guy barely had anything on his feet. From where he was standing, Og was on the outer circumference of the shambles. He stalked to the corner, grabbed the implements, then slapped the dustpan into Zach's hand. "Don't move. Squat when I need a hand."

Adjusting how he held the broom to protect his bad hand, Og swept the sharp shards of glass into the center of the room, then went along the outside perimeter, taking care to reach even where nothing was visible. Couldn't have anyone getting hurt, and there was the idiot mutt. Damn slivers could hurt a dog's paws.

He filled the dustpan, handed it to Zach, who dumped it into the garbage beside him, then silently handed it back to him. He tackled the mashed-up fruit next. He caught the man—Nathan—staring at him in open query.

He wasn't about to explain himself.

That done and thrown out, he strode to the sink, popped the broom in, and opened the tap to clean it all up. He laid the broom back against the wall resolutely, then stood in front of Nathan, who was still hanging on to the squirming dog, who was apparently trying to get itself free and introduce itself to Og.

"Done." He speared Nathan with a glare. "Now, if you want to do business, do you think you could let that big white monster go, take a few minutes, and show me around the place?"

Chapter Six

Nathan

They trudged around the outside of Manor House in silence. Nathan beside Og, his jacket zipped part way up, a copy of the *New York Times* opened to the stock page peeking from an inside pocket.

Og's spicy aftershave struck Nathan's senses and was actually not half bad.

But he was still a jerk.

Og had told them a little of his background, his investments, his gym.

Nathan hadn't been surprised. Yep, a boxer. Made sense. Og dripped sweaty, lickable muscles. Even fully clothed, the guy was well-built, and took care to keep himself that way. Along with his easy confidence, he was a looker. But Nathan had shut that all down. A truly beautiful body and all that self-assurance meant nothing more than Og was eye candy with money to invest. He'd explained he knew he had an appointment in a couple of days, but had decided to drive up early, see what was going on. Nathan had a feeling Og liked keeping people off balance, and had made the trip to catch them unaware.

The grass beneath the last of the snow was springy, and the ever-present crash of the waves in the bay, merely steps away, filled the cool air.

Nathan took care to keep a wide distance between himself and Og. That display he'd put on in the kitchen didn't make the guy Nathan's buddy, and best as he could tell, Og wasn't really interested in the place. The couple of times Nathan had glanced at Og during the inside tour, his vivid green eyes were taking in every detail of the old home. The sloping floors on the second level, worse on the third. The musty smell in the little self-contained suite on the side. Og hadn't looked happy. Not even mildly impressed. He looked as if he wanted to be as far away as he could get.

Now that they were outside, he was probably noting the crumbling masonry around the base of the old building, the gaps between most of the windows and the framing. The wrap-around porch Nathan loved so much needed painting, as well loose boards needed to be replaced. Some of which he would've gotten done, if Og knew how to read a calendar.

Sure, there was a ton of work that needed to be done, but the bones of the place were good. What Og couldn't feel was the love that still circulated through the old house. Nathan was wrapped up in it. Except for that one room he'd judiciously avoided showing Og, the rest of the house sang with potential. Nathan had learned investors didn't want potential; they wanted a guaranteed win.

"Setting up a little love nest for you and your partner?"

Nathan stared at Og, surprised at the question, which had come out of the blue.

The man's eyes bore into him relentlessly. The color of the dark, springy moss in the little enclave in the forest he'd always escaped to when life had been too much. When he'd been in New York, he'd painstakingly gone over every aspect of that place in his mind's eye, and it had gotten him through.

"Oh, you mean—"

"Yeah. The good-looking dude inside doing your dishes."

"Zach?" Nathan couldn't help but laugh. "He's my best friend, but we're not a couple."

"Oh." Og seemed like he didn't believe him. "Some little lady waiting for you somewhere who's gonna join you here if you get the money to pretty it all up?"

Why the hell was he so interested? Doing his due diligence, or was he…. No. This guy was not gay. Pity.

"No. Zach's planning on staying and renting a room. I'm an artist, and I need a place to work. Got some plans for the space." Plans that were the single thing keeping the blood pumping through his veins this last year. The only reason, except for duty, that kept him alive.

"What kind of plans?"

As if he'd tell him. Open his guts to him. Crack open his chest and invite the slaughter.

They rounded the back corner of the property and a graying, weathered barn appeared in front of them. "Well, they're in the formative stage, but first, I want Manor House to be part of the community again. To integrate. There were some issues when the place was rented, and I want all that to be in the past." He eyed the large structure. "They used to keep a few animals in there, once upon a time. Been empty for years."

Og stopped beside him and perused the building. "You know a lot about the property. Research buff?"

Nathan smiled. "Only the up close and personal kind. Manor House has been in my family many generations. I spent my summers here for most of my childhood."

"Memories are important. Good ones, it sounds like."

Nathan nodded. Those memories were precious, and not up for public consumption or comment. They were his.

But they weren't today.

Today was deadly serious.

"Good to hear. Problem is," Og said, as he bent and poked at the crumbling mortar of the foundation, "memories don't pay the bills, and won't give me a return on my investment."

There it was. The bottom line coming from the man with the money. Like all the others before him.

Og turned toward the bay, and his eyes narrowed as a gentle wind danced along the top of the waves, buffeting them, bringing the scent of kelp and fish with it. Beaches, shells, pretty things. Wood bleached in the sun, starfish so close. An artist's bounty and launching pad.

"Pretty. View's good. Increases resale value."

Sure. That's all that would matter to you..

But Nathan had a sense they were negotiating now. He nodded, stayed quiet.

No resale. This is a family property.

"Chimney needs redoing. Odd symbols up top, but they have that weird country charm, no need to get rid of them." Og's gaze panned down the chimney to the foundation. "I wouldn't be surprised if it's wet in the basement. Old place like this, spring thaw, sometimes floods, it all adds up. You're probably working on that already."

Nathan's chest deflated and a sinking feeling filled his gut. This guy was astute. Nathan had seen the way Og scrutinized the house inside and out.

"Community means a lot in an area like this. You got the right idea integrating. Sometimes, when things are a mess, it's the only thing that gets you through. There's emergency services out here, but you're isolated. Bad storm…" He shrugged. "If your neighbors have a stake in the place or you, they're important, and will help you."

Nathan held Og's gaze, warming to matter-of-fact confidence, and the odd-shaped nose that made him more interesting. Made him seem strong, like he could handle anything that came at him. A wave of need hit him. What would it feel like to be with someone like that?

"Does that mean you…"

Og sucked in a breath, held it, like he wanted to say something but was holding back. "Not smart from a financial perspective. Place is a wreck and needs a huge cash infusion. Time to give it up, Mister Gentael. The plans. All of it."

Energy arced between them and the eighteen inches or so wasn't enough space for Nathan to be able to ignore Og's spicy scent.

"Nathan?"

His mind stalled on that husky voice. Any other time, any other place… give it up? *Sure*. Gladly. Hell yeah. But he was done with all that. He *was*.

He snapped himself out of the momentary fantasy and glared Og. "The starving artist archetype exists for a reason. A lot of us *have* to starve to make our art. About the property, there's a ton of bedrooms in this place, a huge living room, and a big kitchen. The basement— wet as it is—is a write-off at the moment. But with a bit of work, this place can become a hobby farm. We can grow some of our vegetables, make our own food."

"And?"

Clearly Og knew there was more to the story, and knew Nathan was holding back. Og's dark green eyes were unusually bright, indicating interest. In Nathan or the house?

It had been such a long time since he'd felt anything at all, he knew he was misreading the signals, but there was something about this guy that made Nathan want to trust him. As scary as that was, the words spilled out, and his guard came down.

"I want a place where guys that are messed up can come and recover. Contribute. Artists of all types. Masons, metal workers, painters, sculptors…whatever. If some guy wants to pull a Kief Fasset and wants to knit up a storm, more power to him." He paused, feeling like he was allowing some of his blood to leave his body to fuse with another's.

It was time. He needed to create what had been burning in him for so long. The only thing that had given him a reason to move forward.

Then, if he could untangle this horrid mess with his father….

"I want an artist's haven, a getaway, whatever you want to call it. Whoever wants to express himself through art and needs a place to hole himself away from society, if they need time to recover or create, I want this place to be here for them."

He braced himself for the inevitable scoffing, the mocking. This guy was tough, a doer who made money off other people's backs. There's no way he would care about an undertaking like this unless he'd get big bucks in return, and Nathan didn't think a refuge in Refuge Bay was a moneymaking enterprise.

Incredibly, Og didn't snort, or laugh, or share his disdain or disgust. In fact, he seemed more alert, his green eyes brightening. A light seemed to've lit inside the imposing man. How curious.

"The Refuge Bay Artists' Collective, huh? I like it. You know, I think I might—"

His last words were lost as a crash coming from the barn. The awful noise echoed through the air, abruptly discordant in the peaceful surroundings, and then deadly silence.

Chapter Seven

Og

The sound caught Og off guard, but he steeled himself in anticipation of his body and mind's reaction. There wouldn't be a replay of *that*. He'd be on alert, as he normally was, every damn second from now on. Foolishly, he'd been lulled into being relaxed, thinking about a cozy little future here.

To make it worse, the poet gave him a blank look, which turned to shock. Those gorgeous brown, soulful eyes stared at him. Those eyelashes fluttered, and Nathan seemed to reach out to Og. Then he started running, hell-bent, toward the barn.

Og took off after him, determined to get there first. *Protect and serve.*

Nathan got to the barn door first, reached to fling it open. "Careful. You don't know who's in there." Og tried to slam his hand against the door to close it, but he missed. It was too late, swinging wide.

"Don't be crazy," Nathan yelled. "There's no one in here. It had to be the wind."

Og glared at his face, tight and drawn as it was. "Then why are you so worried?"

"I'm not worried." As if to prove his point, Nathan darted abruptly into the dark cavern, and Og stifled the urge to strangle him. If this was how Nathan lived his life, running into danger without a thought for his safety, the guy absolutely needed a protector.

Og moved slowly, taking in absolutely everything. He mapped the area. Sunlight speared the barn, painted the walls and floor in parallel lines through the slatted sides. Hay was scooped up onto the edges into large piles and dusted the floor lightly. Ancient wooden columns spiked upward, holding up the roof and bracing the loft on one side. Enormous hooks hung on the walls. An old tractor, broken down and in pieces, took up one area. Off to the side, in front of them, was a labyrinth of black that snaked off into stalls and, after that, liquid darkness.

"What the hell was that sound?" Nathan's gaze panned around him. "I bet it was over in the work area. There's all kinds of crap there."

Og's mind was combing through all the possibilities. Peril could be lurking anywhere.

Behind every mound of hay, behind every wall, could be...

Once again, the poet didn't think. He ran past a partition into the dark. "Over here."

Og followed, ready for anything. There was a workbench, a mess of old tools, grease, boxes, and junk. But on the floor, glinting in the sun, was a huge jumble of glass, metal, and crushed tin.

***

Nathan

"What the hell?" Nate grimaced, eying the stuff on the floor. "There was nothing here yesterday. I came in to get a crowbar."

Og stared at the odd configuration and moved in closer. His brawny shoulder brushed Nathan, who didn't jolt away.

Og's spicy scent traveled through Nathan's body, and at the same time he noticed Og didn't seem to mind a bit of body contact while Nathan totally should. Og was the enemy. He held all the power, because he held the money.

Being touched, even accidently, by this bull of a man felt good, like coming home. Like he'd always been beside him, exciting him, yet his presence was reassuring. Og radiated strength and power, and continued to stay close while investigating the scene.

"Huh," Og said. "Take a look at that string."

Nathan's gaze followed a pale string attached to the mess, then threaded off into the distance. It was so well done that if you didn't take the time to follow it, you wouldn't see the route. He took a few steps forward, following it as it disappeared under a partition.

"Holy hell," Nathan muttered. "I wonder…" He started toward the edge of the wooden wall.

Og sputtered. "You can't… oh, for fuck's sake." Og jumped into action, pushing Nathan back with a strong arm, then moved ahead, disappearing into the dark.

An abrupt yell followed by a huge boom, then a resounding bang, and more noises.

A high-pitched shriek pierced the air. "Lemme go, you creep."

Nathan moved forward past the divider, then stopped at the scene before him.

Og was embroiled in an altercation with an intruder, his face flushed from exertion as he wrestled the stranger, who was clad in a sweatshirt with a hoodie concealing his face. Nathan tried to jump in but the two were crazy. Og was so big, and the other so much smaller and slight, and able to writhe and dart because of it. Og kept wincing, especially when he grasped the intruder with his left hand.

On the ground, off to the side, Nathan's gaze flicked over another mess. Opened tins, discarded spoons. A threadbare pillowcase. Matches. Battery starter, clamps. A thick blanket. Over on a bale of hay a pair of small pink underwear hung, flashing a huge grinning Beauty and the Beast.

The shocked words fell from Nathan's lips. "A girl?"

Like he'd been clutching a hot potato, Og's arms, which had finally gotten into a solid deadlock around the intruder, fell fully off, as though he'd been hugging a statue that had become electrified. "You're a girl?" he bellowed.

The intruder made good use of her freedom, grabbed a cast-iron fry pan from a pile of junk, slugged Og with it, and ran.

"Ugh." The big man took the hit, folded, then miraculously unfolded, and yelled at Nathan. "Don't let her get away. You don't know what she'll do."

"Like beat you up?" But Og was right. With a few quick strides, Nathan grabbed her sweatshirt as she stumbled, and then yanked her to him, folded his arms around her, and the intruder seemed subdued.

"Lemme go. Lemme go," she shouted.

Nathan tightened his hold. It seemed like all he'd been doing today was subduing the crazy. A dog first, now a waif who'd seemed much more powerful and big a few minutes ago, but now that he looked at her, he saw all the extra clothes padding her. Layers and layers of them. "Hold on. Stop struggling and tell me who you are and what are you doing here?"

"Lemme go." The girl tried to wrench herself away, but Nathan felt it coming and held on even tighter.

"I can do this forever, missy. If I did get tired, my buddy over there will take over. Do you really want that?"

"Ew, you creep." Her voice was raw. "Lemme go. Lemme go."

Og appeared in front of them, still rubbing the contact point where the ancient fry pan had landed. Nathan saw Og's lips twitch for a moment, then he was stern again and fixed the girl with a terrifying look. If Nate didn't know better, he'd shiver in his boots too.

"He's right," Og said matter-of-factly. "We can deliver you to the authorities or we can get your details while you're eating a hamburger and a pile of fries, and drinking a chocolate milkshake or a frosty Coke. Option A or B?"

Nathan watched her face in the reflection of a rusty-edged mirror hanging on the opposite barn wall. The badly cut, choppy hair, the dirty face, and the hungry gleam, which killed him. He felt like a voyeur, her look so intense and soul-deep. She widened her eyes as Og tempted her with food. And the word option wasn't lost on the girl. A tiny bit of fear left her face.

Clever man. The guy knew people.

Nathan had always been slow in that way. Trusting people too easily, being hurt, or more like having his soul raked through nail beds each time until he'd decided he wouldn't trust anymore. Which really wasn't a good life strategy. Trust too much, then shrivel your soul and heart to the size of a dried pea. Kinda stupid, but it was the best he had.

Having seen Og in action, Nathan had to admit, he admired the big guy. Not so much a cretin anymore, it seemed.

Brilliant and decent. It was no matter if he wasn't the investor they'd be dealing with, who didn't love the property like Nathan did, he was a decent person.

"Which is it?" Og prodded the recalcitrant kid.

"Fucking hamburger."

Og didn't skip a beat. "Fucking fries, too?"

"Fucking milkshake, too, and fucking Coke."

Og lowered himself onto an old bale of hay and Nathan loosened his hold on the girl. "Excellent," Og said. "First off, name?"

The girl's hazel eyes blazed, and she spat the word, "Trasher."

Og's eyes flicked over the scene of discarded stuff off to their right, then returned to her face. "Oddly appropriate. Rank and serial number?"

"Huh?" Her face distorted as she looked at him with the disgust only a kid could pull off.

He gave up the attempt at late-night movie humor. "Last name. As in whose kid are you, and why did you run?"

She shook her head vehemently. "That's not in the deal. I'm here because I *love* eating out of tin cans and sleeping in shitty barns."

"Gotcha. You're a romantic. Okay, if my friend lets you go, will you stand still? Or run?"

Her eyes screwed up. "Run if I can, ya big dope."

"Funny. I knew that already." He stalked over to the wall, lifted off a rope, then reached around her and tied it in a solid knot.

The ease with which he did it zinged through Nate. Og was totally self-sufficient and seemed to know what to do in any situation. Like in the kitchen, during the inspection, and now.

How did a person become that?

Trasher was throwing ocular death rays at Og, and struggling. "You can't do this."

"Give it a rest." Og sighed. "Listen, kid. The best meal you've had in days is waiting for you, we promise that. You're gonna relax, no danger, and we'll make sure of that, as well. Then, once we've fed you, we'll see about calling the authorities. But in the meantime…"

Nathan could become mesmerized watching Og, but he had to find a way to get this investor back on track. Fulfilling his mission—saving his house and his Army buddies—would kick the deep depression he'd been in its ass.

He needed this to work, and this guy was the key. The only investor who was left standing. It seemed he knew how to handle himself. Handle anything. A good man to have on your side.

But if this guy got all involved with this kid—much as Nathan wanted her sorted out—the deal would be forgotten, and he'd be back to nothing.

Og's strong voice cut in, aimed at the scrawny, unkempt little upstart.

"So, tell us what's going on. We'll do our best to shut up and listen. But know this. We're calling the authorities, and that's nonnegotiable. Got it?

***

Og

Og groaned. This was all he'd needed on a day when he had to wrap up a fast deal. One he could present to Palmer as the community project he required, and have the man finally give Og the job he was desperate for.

From once-in-a-while consultant to steady employee. He needed it. And Michael needed it even more.

Og didn't have time for this. Or for the dude who clearly needed rescuing all the time. He mentally rolled his eyes. He had to extricate himself, fast.

But here was the kid, there was the dude.

The kid stayed silent, and he grabbed her by the neck of her filthy shirt with his bad hand and prisoner-walked her out of the barn into the unexpected wind that had blown up in the short time they'd been inside. He'd deposit her in the kitchen with Zach, they'd figure out the most expedient way to make good on his food promise, and then he'd try to salvage the deal so he could get the hell back to NY.

Nathan had said he was going to stay behind and take a quick look around in the barn. He'd seemed upset, but mainly, he was already too into the kid and rescuing her, not so worried about the barn and their stuff and what she might have done to it.

Stupid. Nice and all, but unrealistic. Obviously the guy was impractical or he wouldn't be trying to resurrect an old house that was in rough shape with no money to do it.

The best thing Og could do with the kid was get her into the hands of the authorities so his business investment—the dreamy, impractical poet—was not sidetracked from his fiduciary duties. Namely doing whatever the hell he had to do to make money, turning a nice profit for himself, and paying Og back, plus the hefty interest on the loan.

"Quit pushing me." The girl yanked him back to the moment at hand as she railed against his hold.

"Then keep moving. Target? Back door over there."

"Fine, Gomer."

A tiny smile curled his lips. How the hell did she know about Gomer Pyle? The dig bounced off him, but it made him wonder about the kind of upbringing she'd had. A 50s sitcom wasn't typical pop culture for a kid her age.

She still wasn't ready to be cooperative. She kept fighting him as they made their way through the yard. He attempted to propel her forward, but she leaned back into his hand, trying to make it harder for him. Which made him push her harder. A little game he couldn't wait to stop playing.

He watched as her dirty, hole-filled sneakers oozed into the muck she seemed intent on stepping in. Most kids avoided puddles. This one avoided dry ground. Telltale wisps of plain brown hair escaped from her baseball cap, flying in all directions in the wind as it picked up around them, sending bits of old snow blowing past them.

A stupid kid who didn't know how lucky she was to have been found by him, or by *I'll be decent no matter what* Nathan, who wore his heart on his sleeve.

The guy was an absolutely open book. In his expression, in the manner in which he regarded this dump of a house, and in the careful way he dealt with the kid. He'd been near shocked by the conspiratorial, duplicitous, and dangerous configuration the kid had set up.

Og had seen stuff like this before. He knew not only was she an expert at avoiding capture, but that she'd have an awful reason to become so proficient at it.

That trap she'd rigged? He'd seen similar in the jungles. Yeah, it was basic, even primitive, but it was a definite bait-and-trap operation.

He felt sweat burst out on the back of his neck. The kid needed to be safe. Every kid needed that. Michael hadn't had that, even with his older brother in the same house.

"Quit pushing." she shouted again. God, she had a set of lungs. Looked to be about seven, barely. "I'm going as fast as I can."

He nudged her, and as he expected, she yelped. "Those dark clouds don't mean things are going to stay peachy keen out here, kid.

We need to get in and under cover since it's gonna pour, and I don't want you getting wet and catching a cold."

"Wet? Seriously. You're worried about me getting wet? I've been living in alleyways, and in that stink-bomb of a barn." The kid made that thousand-percent disgusted noise, and spat for good measure.

Tough little thing. Survival either molded people into what this tough nut had become, or it buckled them.

Og found himself coming under the spell of the child, the house, and the peninsula. Even though it was attached to the mainland, this place seemed like a small world of its own—a thousand miles from civilization. Far from the hustle and bustle he normally loved. He had to get back to that quick 'cause he was falling.

This place was getting under his skin like a tick from the forest.

It wasn't only the house and the bay, and this incredible land that stood stalwart against the ocean and the breakers and the winds he knew would be merciless. His eyes panned up the solid brick line of the dwelling, up to that odd chimney. The crazy metalwork on top. The collection of bricks that seemed to say, *I've been here three hundred years and I'll be here another three. I won't let those down that have asked for safe harbor behind my walls. I'll protect them and shield them, and if you want protection too, step inside.*

Og shook his head. He was reading way too much into this dump, and yeah, way too much into the slight man with the big eyes, and the determination to fight hard for his big dream, no matter what it took.

They were at the kitchen door now. He pushed the girl in with a gentle shove.

"In ya go, kid."

***

Nathan

Og had been clear as he'd whispered his orders. *Make sure there's no kerosene uncapped anywhere. Make sure the barn is safe.* His hot breath on Nathan's ear had sent shivers down his spine. He was still vibrating from the unintended caress.

Nathan moved into the stall, one over, where there had been horses only a few years back. Nothing prize-winning on their little peninsula. Nothing glamorous. But everyday animals that had been loved well and had a good life here. The wooden wall between the two stalls came up halfway between floor and ceiling, and it was there the child had made her camp. Wider, yet cozy, he would've chosen here. It's a spot a kid would think was like a little bedroom even though the barn was in terrible shape.

She'd gathered up as much clean hay as she could, and created a bed for herself. Beside the bed lay a jumble of old harnesses and bits, and, most interestingly, an old horse blanket.

She'd found Livy's old blanket, and it was thick, which lay beside the makeshift bed. Perhaps she did that so if she reached her hand out in the dark, she could touch the rough weave and find some sort of comfort in feeling cloth instead of straw or wooden floorboards.

There was something dark, lumpy, and large on the other side of the blanket in the shadows. He moved closer, bent to look, and saw a saddle. The leather practically black from wear, smooth in the concave curve of it. *Huh.* The girl loved horses.

She was definitely a runaway, another problem for him to solve as quickly as possible in a huge, long list of problems, but knowing she loved horses warmed his heart. It made him wonder about their little interloper. She had a mouth on her that would embarrass sailors, and eyes that had widened at the promise of real food, but she had a soft spot for horses.

***

Og

Zach was at the deep sink, doing dishes in soapy, steaming water. He'd gotten dressed and sported black skinny jeans and a rumpled polo with gold and hunter green mini stripes showing off nice tanned arms. He lifted an eyebrow wryly as Og shoved the girl into the kitchen. "You've been busy."

"You have an intru—" He winced at his choice of words, coughed quickly and corrected himself. "A resident in that huge chaos of a building that's masquerading as a barn out there."

Zach's eyebrow stayed steady. "I see." He gave the girl a once-over, then glanced at Og with a wordless question.

Og gazed at him, telegraphing the important info silently. *She needs help. Food. It appears...we're it.*

Zach threw the dishcloth into the water. Suds flew. He grabbed a damp tea towel from the counter beside him and started furiously rubbing his hands. "Cookies. She'll want cookies."

Interesting. Guy had shifted into protector mode again. The dude was definitely a bodyguard. He'd seen it with Nathan, now with the kid.

Zach opened the cupboard's skinny, tall door in front of him, stared into the dull, colorless interior and yanked out a plate, then fixed his gaze on the waif. "Pooh Bear plate work for you?"

The waif scowled. "Kinda kiddie, don'tcha think?"

"Right. That one's mine then. One of the Disney princesses then?"

Og watched the unfolding play with interest. Trasher rolled her eyes dramatically, but not before he caught the automatic wince she tried to hide so quickly. An offer to be a princess met with disdain in her little soul.

"As if." She scowled.

"Seeing as these plates were salvaged from a local yard sale, our pickings are rather slim. Oh, wait." Zach pulled one from the bottom of the pile, causing a clatter. "Here's one that's more in keeping with your personality." He flashed it in front of her with a flourish. The metal hooded figure of Darth Vader with a sabre firmly grasped in his right hand.

She tried not to react to the villain, but Og saw the pleasure in her eyes for a scant flash before she shut it all down again and feigned boredom.

"Whatever. Where are the fucking cookies already?"

He couldn't help himself. He shoved down the laughter, then tapped her lightly upside the back of her head.

She jerked away quickly as if he'd really hit her.

His stomach plummeted, and his jaw hardened.

An old memory flashed behind his eyes. Gargoyles overhead, their cruel faces carved into wood that practically pulsed with their brutality. Curved talons and claws extending toward him, angling for a vicious swipe. He forced his mind quickly back to the task at hand, and recognized as tough as she was, and seemed, she was still a kid.

Kids needed rules and a framework. This one wouldn't respond to teddy bears and hugs. So tough love coming right up.

"First rule of your stay here, kid. The *f word* will not come out of your mouth."

Her face morphed from shock to complete disbelief. "Well hell."

Og shut down the laugh bubbling up from his gut. "That's gone too."

"*Shit*. Do I at least get to keep damn?"

"Shit? Becomes sugar. Or any other sh-word you prefer. Damn is now darn or doohickey."

"Good go—" she started, then stopped. "Grief." She shook her head. "Whatever." She eyed Zach and her face settled into a pout. "If it's okay to use the C word, can I have those? Or maybe I better not. That might be a banned word too." She looked in Og's direction. "Where are the little mixed-up bundles of flour and sugar?"

"Here." Without missing a beat, Zach unceremoniously deposited the cookies on Darth and flicked a glance to her face.

It was unsettling how fast her little hands grabbed them then stuffed them into her mouth. An expression of pleasure washed over her as no doubt the sugar hit her system.

"Good?" Zach asked the question quietly.

She looked up at him with an angelic expression. Now she'd thank him, or smile. Instead, they got, "Bitchin'."

Og blinked. "Kid. That one's gone, too."

Her face transformed into that of a tiny soldier. "Serious?"

"Oh yeah. From now on, you're fine, amazing, awesome, but never *that* word."

"Whatever."

He scrutinized her. "You sure? Got all that straight?"

"Yeah," she muttered as she reached for another cookie.

Damn it all. He didn't want to call the authorities and release her into their care. He knew the system sucked, but she was young, homeless, and clearly the victim of abuse. She needed the kind of help these two guys couldn't and shouldn't provide.

That this was none of his damn business danced around the edge of his mind. Not this cute little guerrilla of a kid, not that poet artist out in the barn with the dreamy eyes and the obviously wounded heart, not this wreck of a house that somehow called to Og. None of it was his concern. He had an investment to make, and a job to secure so he could take care of his brother, Michael.

Og needed to nail down the deal and get the hell out of here. Wrap it all up then leave and let them fend for themselves, forget he'd ever met any of them.

He had to get back to his only reason for doing this shit.

Finding Michael, and keeping him alive.

Chapter Eight

Nathan

Nathan walked quickly to the house, head bent against the wind. Looked like old Jonesy's bones had known what the hell they were thinking. A storm was kicking up, big time.

He shook his head. The kid was a thorn in his plans, for sure. They'd bring in the authorities to deal with it. He had to admit, though, seeing Og with her, and the way he handled the situation, had been hot. Nathan had always been drawn to the strong, masterful type, but he couldn't go there. Men like that were too heavy-handed, and didn't have the type of heart he needed.

They were probably in there fighting like cats and dogs. He was almost at the door, and he steeled himself then yanked it open, and there they all were. Lights on against the dark sky, he found a domestic scene: the kid at the old wooden table, swinging her dirty-socked feet as she sat, a heap of cookies in front of her on the Pooh plate, and Darth Vader menacing from another plate on which was nothing but crumbs. She was making a dent in the pile, and had left huge splotches of mud of the floor.

Og sat on the floor, his back against the wall, knees bent, his hands resting on them. Strong, powerful hands. Not looking at a phone, or talking, quiet and alert. Zach was on the floor too, over by the sink, an array of things around him to put away from a big cardboard box. Plastics. He was leaning forward into the dark reaches of the bottom cupboard, muttering.

Who had cancelled the runaway rerun and replaced his family with *Modern Family*?

As if to interrupt his reverie, Zach moaned. "Too *damn* much Tupperware. It's got a life of its—"

"Why does *he* get to swear? *Shit*. You'd think it's a free country and child labor is illegal. And then—" Her words cut off as Og's foot flew up and kicked the leg of her chair.

"See what I mean?" she spat at Nathan with disgust. "You say a normal word—it's a bodily function for god's sake—" she turned quickly in preparation for the kick, which didn't come, "and you get beaten for frig's sake. Ogre. Pri...*piranha*."

"Yeah, you can call me Shrek." Og looked up at Nathan, and he felt the electric charge that seemed to streak through him whenever Og gave him his undivided attention. "Everything okay in the barn?"

"Yeah. Notice the weather?" He scanned the kitchen and noted the curtains at the small kitchen window were drawn. "Zach?"

"Some of our current visitors don't like seeing the high winds." His head bobbed toward the kid. "Still building?"

"It's worse."

Og suddenly came to life, standing up in a fluid, swift motion. Even that seemed masterful, the way he moved with such purpose. What a weird jumble of feelings Nathan experienced. He hated Og's power over Nathan's future and the plans that meant so much to him, but he found himself drawn to the beast of a man. Too drawn.

That body. The strength rippling through him. Confidence, and not as an outer garment, put on, but in him. It wound right through his body. Through his damn sinews. Og was sure of himself and his abilities. His capabilities. Nate couldn't imagine a situation where he wouldn't know exactly what to do.

Stray thought: it'd amazing to have someone like that in Nathan's life.

Og grasped the back of Trasher's chair with both hands. "Listen, it's been a blast and all, but now that you're back, it's time for me to leave." He gave Trasher a serious glance. "Kid needs two keepers at any one time." At this Trasher's face contorted, and he responded immediately with an answering grimace.

The two were getting along famously.

Og angled his wrist, copped a glance at his watch. Even that, with the old-fashioned circular dial, he wore so well on that wrist. That forearm. God.

Stop looking.

"Gotta go. I'm already past schedule. I'll be in touch after I check some figures. If you're willing to make some adjustments, we might be able to do business."

"Adjustments?" Even while Nathan didn't want him to leave, the word hit him hard. He had a vision, a plan. He didn't want someone else's imprint on this place.

"Yeah. Adjustments. Business plan for starters, cash flow statements. The basics."

They weren't quite done. Okay, he hadn't even started.

The big man continued as he moved toward the front hallway. "I've got a few projects on the go, and if you're not into it, I got others to invest in. No skin off my nose, if this one ain't a starter."

Nathan bristled. Damn money men. They'd say whatever they needed to get the best deal. He felt the bile rise in his throat, the familiar clench in his stomach. The words dropped leaden from his mouth. "Well, if this isn't going to suit you, then by all means—"

The kid piped up. "Yeah, yeah. Good one."

All three pivoted to her. "What?" The word popped from Nathan.

"He's playing you. He wouldn't have hung out for another half hour waiting for you to come back in from the stink palace if he didn't like it here. And you."

Trasher caught Og's stern look, dipped her chin for a moment, then pushed through again, this time with heat. "I been around. I know grifts. You're playing him. You're interested. You can beat me or shove crap down my throat, pull out my toenails. Stick nails up my nose. But I know what you're thinking. You can't fool me."

Og's stare turned deadly. The muscles in his frame tightened, and for a moment Nathan thought *he's going to blow*. When things didn't go Og's way, he transformed into a crazy man. Masterful meant mean. Always had.

Then, calm as can be, Og said, "Is that why the...ogre stuck around?"

Nathan watched as Og took a couple of steps to her, the lines of his body rigid. One more step and he'd....

Og stopped. He reached toward the child, and with large fingers, rumpled her hair with one quick flick under the cap. Then he rubbed the top with a quick, affectionate skim. He exhaled a quiet burst of air, as in... *busted*.

"Kid's got a clue." His gaze turned uncharacteristically soft for a scant second, then it was as if it never happened, the change was so abrupt. He was all business again.

He fixed Nathan with a glare that felt like it was going to spear him to the opposite wall, it was so intense. "Call the powers that be. Get this kid where she needs to go." He gave her a different look, one that seemed to envelop her. "Safe."

He zipped his leather jacket up in one fluid swipe and quickly adjusted the copy of the *New York Times* inside. "But first, order in. McDonald's and greasy fries. They got a delivery thing going. Saw it on the way in. Few miles back, but it should extend to here." He smiled. "Extra on the salt. Don't forget the milkshake. Supersize the lot." He dug in his pocket, pulled out way too many bills, and threw them on the table. "My share. Get her whatever she wants." His voice took on a grumbly tone. "Give her something else to chew her mouth around than those damn words. Kid talks too much."

He glanced at his watch again and his whole body seemed ready to catapult into action. Every cell vibrating, focused on movement. To leave.

There went those crazy feelings again.

"Remember. Business plan, cash flow, or it's a no. Gotta go. Be in touch."

He strode through to the front hallway, his boots making a heavy clomping sound all the way. The front door opened, slammed abruptly, and Og was gone.

Chapter Nine

Nathan

"Well, that was fun. Jerk likes to be in charge." Zach nodded to Nathan. "Check with Sally, maybe there's another investor. We don't need his kind."

He dove in to the fridge, came out with a hunk of pale yellow cheese. "Gouda, kid. When you're old enough to have a good Malbec wine, you whip one of these out and serve it to your special someone and they'll love you for it." He plunked the wedge beside the cookies, brandished a small, sterling silver cheese knife and stuck it in the top. "Need something to balance the sugar in those little piles of flour, sugar, and baking powder."

Trasher eyed the cheese, then grabbed another handful of cookies off the Pooh plate before depositing them on Darth. "As if you'd know anything about guy-girl stuff." She stuffed another animal cookie into her mouth, chomping loudly.

The kid needed to get some table manners.

"What do you mean?" Zach eyed her. Trasher merely kept inhaling the cookies as if he hadn't spoken. He pulled a chair out from under the table and sat on it backwards. "Stop stuffing for one second. What gives?"

She motioned between Zach and Nathan. "You're not into females, either of you." Her segue to more important matters was unbroken. "Where's the burger I was told I'd get?"

Nate leaned against the counter and watched them for a few minutes. The energy in the room was picking up. The burst of confusing loneliness he'd felt when Og had left didn't make sense, and didn't feel good.

He was here in this gorgeous old house, hoping for the money to give it a makeover so he can offer the same to himself and men like him. That was his bigger purpose. Not pining over a guy who'd blown in, made demands, then blown out.

"I'll call McDonald's. We'll get the biggest kid special going."

"Kid special?" Trasher whined. "Pukey little burger?" She pushed the empty Darth plate away from her with disgust. "Triple bacon burger, man-size, extra cheese. Side of cheese on the side. Fries. Lots of them. Ketchup. Those little packets of vinegar. Apple pie. Coke. Milkshake, chocolate. Maybe some chocolate wrapped up in those little foil things."

He'd have said something about her demanding tone, simply for form's sake, if for nothing else than to pass on some good values and a life lesson.

Nathan had caught that awful, bottomless glint in her eye. She'd gorged on cookies, but was still crazy desperate to have a burger and fries. She obviously couldn't bear to think there wouldn't be enough. That she'd have to stop before she was full.

Clearly, the poor kid had learned to do without a lot in life, and the thought made him sick deep and hard, right into his gut.

He knew what that felt like and couldn't bear to know someone else might feel that way. Especially a little girl.

"Man-size it is." He pressed the button on his cell, then was surprised when he was met with dead air. Shit. He'd missed an emergency message, from five minutes earlier. "What the?"

"What is it?" Zach's head turned sharply.

Before he could answer, he heard the blast of the front door busting open, the slam of it whipping hard against the wall in the front hallway.

"Men." The voice his soul already seemed to know all too well carried to the kitchen easily. "Batten down the hatches."

The man who'd left scarcely ten minutes ago appeared in the kitchen doorway once more. His face was ruddy from exertion, his tawny hair a wild mess, and dead leaves fell from his jacket. "It's bad out there, and it's barreling this way. Everything secure?"

Nathan and Zach stood and went into action. "Outside cellar door's got to be fastened. On it." Zach ran from the room.

"Barn's got to be latched properly. I'll do it." They couldn't afford to lose a barn door. They couldn't afford what they already had to repair, let alone extra.

"I'll help. Stay here." Og looked at Trasher. It was both an order and a plea, tossed at the little girl by the big man. And she seemed to know its import.

Trasher, wide-eyed, nodded.

Og called to her, "Stay safe," then ran after Nathan into the storm.

***

Og

Nathan ran in front of Og, covering his eyes from flying debris, the sand and dirt whipping through the air as the winds hit him. He yelled, "It's open."

Og strained to see. The big, weather-chipped barn door was flapping wildly, slamming against the side of the barn.

"I'll get it." Nathan reached it, grabbed the edges, and pushed hard against the wind to get it back into place. He'd get a few feet, then the wind would gust up ferociously and slam him back.

Og reached him, grabbed the edge of the door, forcing Nathan to move toward the building. "Hold it. Together, on my count. One, two… three."

Together, they held it. Then, striding forward, battling the elements, they pushed the door into the wind, until… slam. Og shoved the iron bar into place, securing it quickly.

"Let's go." He ran to the house, but realized there was no one beside him. Pivoting, he saw Nathan still slammed against the side of the barn, turned away from the buffeting blasts, gulping in big gulps of air, the barn holding him up.

Og's brow furrowed, and ran back, clocking the fear in Nathan's eyes. Og looped his arm around Nathan's shoulder. "Come on, buddy. It's us. Together. Let's go." He looked into wind-dazed eyes, saw the swirl of brown with gold flecks. The guy had used up most of his strength, it seemed. How could that be?

Didn't matter. He'd get him safe. "Trust me." He saw the answering *help me* in Nathan's eyes, felt him face the wind, and draw closer to his side.

With a firm grip on his shoulders, they took off together, Og pulling him along. They stumbled back until the kitchen door miraculously opened, and Zach yanked them both inside into the warmth.

***

Og

"You coulda been hurt," Trasher burst out. "What were you thinking?"

Og threw his jacket onto a pile of boxes against the wall, shaking on the inside but keeping it together. "Investments need to be protected, little girl. Let that be a lesson for you. You own something, you got to be ready to take care of it, no matter what comes up. It's yours."

Trasher's eyes were still wide, terror circulating in them. And he remembered... he was dealing with a small child. Not an adult, and hell, as evidenced by Nathan's *moment*, grown-ups froze and stuttered too. Even with military training it still happened. He'd seen it often enough in Iraq.

No need to add to her burdens. The life lesson had already been communicated. Responsibilities are important, and are to be discharged. No matter what. His gaze softened. The kid didn't have to learn that yet. Not this moment. Not in the midst of adrenaline pumping through her tiny frame, with no security in her world, and being shut in with three guys who were complete strangers.

He reached over, ruffled her hair. "We're okay, kid. No need to worry."

She looked at him with a terrified expression, then threw herself into a kitchen chair and stared at the table.

"Where the hell did all that blow up from?" Zach grabbed the tea kettle and poured boiling water into a ceramic teapot. Gently, he pushed a mug and a package of hot chocolate in front of Trasher, along with a bag of tiny marshmallows, almost empty, but not quite. He aimed his next question at Og. "How did you get back here?"

"I got a hundred yards when the 'Stang was stopped by a tree. Landed right in front of me, wedged me in. I ran back for shelter and damn lucky I've got heft. If I'd've been ten pounds lighter, the wind would have picked me up and thrown me into the bay."

Og crossed to the sink and whipped open the curtain shrouding the little window and saw trees bending in the storm's fury, dirt and dead grass, small branches hurtling by. He sank into a chair. "Not going anywhere tonight, and looks like the ruffian ain't either. We'll all have to settle in."

Zach glanced over, clearly disapproving the turn of events. "I'll go see about that loose window sash on the third floor. Keep an eye on…" He flicked a glance at Nathan, then stared at Og pointedly. "…things."

Og rolled his eyes as Zach exited the kitchen.

Trasher near shouted, clearly trying to sound strong, "You guys got a ladies room around here or am I supposed to make like an animal and whizz on the—"

"There," Nathan interjected, pointing. "Over there. It's tiny and squishy inside, but it's a couple of steps up from a tree trunk. Or an outhouse."

"An out what?"

Nathan shook his head and grinned with a roll of his eyes. "Go."

She pushed out the chair with a squeak against the old linoleum and marched, with purposeful dignity like a little queen on a red carpet framed by cheering crowds, to the warped door, went in, slammed and locked it. Loudly.

With Trasher and Zach out of the room, silence hung like a shroud. Surprisingly, Og was uncomfortable, which was unusual, and he searched for the reason. The bodyguard didn't care for him, that was clear. But poet-dude, he was different. He wore his vulnerability. The storm overwhelmed him, and the way he'd taken care of the kid…he was kind in a way that said he'd suffered.

"You're a liar." Nathan's voice, gentle yet barely audible, had pierced the silence.

"Huh?"

"I said, you're a liar. You like to hide all that away, don't you?"

Og was taken aback. "Hide all what away?"

Nathan scrutinized him, and for one moment Og felt…naked. Something he hadn't felt for years.

"Whatever's going on, deep inside that you're fighting, it comes out. When you're dealing with the girl, or when you're caught off guard, when you have to use that hand that hurts all time…I can see it. There's something you care about badly that makes you…weak."

Nathan stared at him with those gorgeous caramel eyes. "It scares you to death at the same time you have incredible resolve." Nathan shook his head, and understanding moved in his eyes. "It's hard loving someone or something that much."

Og sat, stunned, without a quick response. No one had ever seen that, ever. He knew for a fact he'd hidden it deep. By all the comments on how callous he could be…even the guys at the gym hadn't seen it, and they liked him.

This shattered soul with a poet's eyes made him.

Holy shit. For a long, delicious moment, tension leaked out of him. If only he could share what was going on with someone. Someone decent, someone caring. Someone who'd have his back, and in so doing, Michael's.

Og couldn't let his guard down. He scanned Nathan, leaning on the antique sideboard in the old kitchen. Cute, pensive. Thoughtful eyes. This guy right there. He was damn dangerous.

"Ha." He shook his head, exaggerated the motion, then shrugged. "No harm done. Doesn't mean a thing. Good story, though." The back door shuddered in its frame. Og threw a quick glance to it. "We've got more important things to worry about right now."

Zach came back as Trasher exited the bathroom, and comically, they almost bumped into each other. Trasher hauled back about the time Zach did. They looked each other up and down, then Zach moved back, let her go first. She marched back to her chair, keeping a wary eye on him.

Zach poured hot water into four mugs, tore open the package of hot chocolate and deposited it into Trasher's. "Stir it." Continuing to no one in particular, he said, "Sash is secured, so that's done. Anything interesting happen while I was gone?"

"Nope. Not a damn thing," Og stated. "I'm starved, and I think the kid needs feeding, too."

He pulled out a heap of cookies from a box sitting by the decimated first cookie box, deposited them on her plate, and put the rest on a napkin for the rest of them. He settled back, and even though the chair was standard issue, second-hand store wooden, he let his body relax into it as if it were the plushest recliner welcoming him.

He was determined not to think of what had transpired between him and the man who'd seen into his damn soul as if it were the easiest thing in the world to manage.

"Let's figure out grub, men. I'm not going any damn where tonight." He tilted his head at Thrasher. "You've got company."

Chapter Ten

Nathan

They'd made a quick meal of scrambled eggs, hot dogs, and a tomato salad, which Zach whipped up, along with a loaf of heavy, brown rye bread Og had saved from his car. Zach had given the orders, and curiously, Og hadn't said a word or pulled rank. Zach had run a compelling commentary, telling Og they had Livy down the road to thank for the tomatoes and Nellie and Bill by the bay in their house for the eggs.

Now they were deciding sleeping arrangements. With this big hunk of man-flesh in the house. Nathan was mortified and expectant at the same time.

"I can sleep anywhere. Don't go to any fuss for me." Og checked his phone again.

"There's Nathan's room, somewhat furnished, on the second floor. Trasher can sleep there. He hasn't slept in it yet." Zach had finished up the dishes and was pouring a steaming cup of tea for everyone in the big mugs. "She'll be safe there. My room's down here, off the front hallway." His gaze skittered from Nathan to Og. "There's a few other bedrooms on the second. I'm sure you can both figure out a way to get some sleep up there."

Great. Sharing a floor, in the dark, with *him*?

And almost as bad was that *the room*—his old studio, his sacred space—was there. Seeing as the house had stayed in the family and there was an abundance of bedrooms, they hadn't bothered clearing it out. He'd originally been given the worst room, even all those years ago, for his studio—the walls were cracking and the floor was lifting—which had played into his lack of enthusiasm for getting into cleaning the studio.

He should've thrown everything out already. Hell, burned it all. It was a billion percent clear he'd never lift a brush again. That was carved in stone. The family all knew it too.

But the room had been kept intact, which shouldn't mean anything except he was a lazy housekeeper. At any rate, he'd shut it off until he could deal with it. No one was allowed in, though Zach had earned the privilege, once. Nathan would have to keep Og away from the studio.

"Wouldn't it be best for you to let Og have your room down here?" Nathan turned to Og. "You want to be close to one of the doors, in case—"

"In case his Mustang comes calling and rings the front doorbell? Come on. Og's already said he'll be fine with anything. And my room's...mine. You know that."

Yeah, he knew that. Zach needed stability. He'd chosen that room for reasons that meant he really needed it.

The die was cast. Nathan and Og would be sharing the second floor. The man who was irritating the hell out of him, yet still crazily drawing him in, would be sharing sleeping space with him, and it felt too intimate.

Og stretched, then rose. "Well, I'll head on up then, if that's settled. Hope you have a working bath up there?"

"Claw-foot tub, old toilet. Fixtures are a bit rusty but clean. Even the rust is spotless. Nathan scrubbed it, and he's amazing."

Nathan watched as Og's gaze licked over him. He started at Nathan's face, dropped to his chest, slid lower, than back up to his face, which had warmed and was probably red. Og's voice held a shrug, but Nathan knew better. "Be interesting finding out."

Chapter Eleven

Og

Og was behind the little girl on the staircase as their tiny convoy made their way up to the second floor. She jolted and he almost lost his cookies. Literally. The plate heaped with them lurched in his grip as Trasher bellowed, "Ewww."

He growled, "This ain't no Victorian thriller, kid. What the heck are you howling about?"

"It's dark. I don't like it. Creepy."

Nathan called back from his position in the lead. "The light switch at the bottom doesn't work. But the one up top does. Hang in there."

Trasher was defiant. "Do you know, like, that's all I've ever heard, all my life? Hang in there. It'll get better. Tomorrow is another day." She mounted two more of the ancient steps slowly, then made her dramatic pronouncement, "I'm waiting."

The laugh rumbled in Og's gut, but he bit it back. Somehow it seemed wrong to let her know how funny she was. She was such an actress, and damn, she was good. Completely believable. Seven or eight, going on thirty-eight.

"Here we are." Nate flicked on the switch. Ghostly swirls of light emanated from the ancient fixtures along one side of the wide hallway. A large, rectangular window at the end framed the indigo sky, and moonlight flash-framed the tree limbs outside that were thrashing wildly in the storm.

They made their way up the rest of the staircase, and Trasher went into the bathroom for a sponge bath. A few minutes later she emerged with, "Multo cree-eepy." She stood, layered in the three oversize T-shirts they'd insisted she wear for warmth. "You guys listen to me. No good will come of this. It's been done before. *This is a movie.*"

Nathan's gaze met Og's over her scruffy little head, and a smile lit in them. A crazy, weird, and temporary form of parenting. Soft sentiments of secrets shared pulsed between them. Og felt it not in real time, as they'd say in the military, but a scant half-second later, and his heart fucking flipped. Warmth spread through his chest, and his cock twitched.

"Where the hell am I sleeping?"

"Over here." Nate led them into a room close to the staircase. "Come on."

A sparse effort had been made to make the room look homey. Old, dark, marked-up wooden floors, plus one faded, braided rug lay in front of the yesteryear bed, also made of dark wood.

Nathan switched on a small bedside lamp and drew the covers back. "Zach made this room up for me as soon as we got here, but I haven't slept in it yet." He looked around at the old dresser. It had a few trinkets on it, and he seemed lost in memory for a moment. He patted the sheet. "In you get."

Surprisingly, she had no words, but leapt in. She jumped onto the bed, and it creaked under her weight. She wiggled, then stuck her feet deep under the covers, laid her arms rigidly at her side, and looked up at Nathan.

It twisted Og's heart.

"Oh, so now we expect tucking-in services?" Nathan smiled, his voice gentle, and Og realized why the whole tableau stopped him in his tracks. Stopped his breath, momentarily.

Nathan was happy. His face lit up, and it made him more tempting. Og couldn't take his eyes off him.

Suddenly, without any fanfare, the kid turned off. Her eyes closed and bam, she was asleep. Of course she'd be tired, given all she'd been through. Being found, making her way among three men she'd never met before, and she'd done a damn good job of it.

Other worrisome thoughts rattled around in his head like how long since she'd slept in a real bed. While cozy for a night or two, hay didn't hold a candle to a real bed, all those comforters tucked around her. From some aunt, Nathan had murmured.

Og acknowledged this moment meant something. Too much.

She mumbled, and Nathan, who'd been staring at her, lost in some dream world of his own, bent quickly, placed his ear to her lips, then straightened. "Yeah, you're right, kid." He tucked her in more fervently, making sure she was covered. Even if this old house was semi-fixed up, cold air or drafts were inevitable until the windows could be replaced.

Nathan motioned Og out of the room, the tiny light still on.

"What did she say?"

Nathan grinned. "The truth."

"And that is?"

"You *owe* me."

Chapter Twelve

Nathan

For fuck's sake. Was the man some kind of superhuman who didn't need to use the bathroom?

Nathan had grabbed a room down the hallway. The old lumpy couch wasn't inviting, but it was all he had, and seeing as he didn't have to lie on the hardwood floor, he supposed he should be grateful. The last two nights he'd fallen asleep on the kitchen floor, head on a heap of old newspapers.

This was better, though barely. He'd insisted Og take the room two doors down from Trasher, where there was a decent mattress on the floor.

The thought of Og, merely a few feet away, kept Nathan awake. He wondered if in slumber Og looked peaceful, and if that constant scowl disappeared. Considering what Og slept in, and that maybe he was naked, made Nathan's cock surge to life. The long day, the scant amount of sleep last night, none of it seemed to matter. He breathed in a shuddery breath, imagined Og's raw scent, his inviting body, mixed with that haunting spicy cologne he wore, and sleep eluded him.

Not for the first time, he thought it was too bad Og was an investor. Nothing could happen between them. Their relationship had to remain strictly business. Which was too bad since getting in bed with Og was an invitation Nathan would accept even knowing in the morning he'd be splintered. The man was so masculine, and would take control in every way possible. Even his pain-in-the-ass attitude that he knew best about everything pissed Nathan right off, yet somehow he believed Og knew best. Nathan would give over in bed, and Og would have him any way he wanted. Nathan shuddered at the same time his cock got harder.

To give over and allow himself to be taken care of by a strong, capable man was enticing, Nathan had to remember the truth: he was alone. Sure, Zach helped him, but being alone was how Nathan knew he had to lead his life. Being with someone soul deep in every way was not for everyone. He'd come to that realization about himself. Not that he liked it, but it was something he'd come to accept.

What he really needed now was to get his mission accomplished. He had to be more like Og. Make a goddamn decision and act on it. At the forefront of that thought was to clear out the studio and get rid of all those dreams. Burn them.

The canvases might exist in form, but for all intents and purposes, they were gone. It had been hard enough to keep Og from opening the door when he'd looked in each room, but Nathan pulled rank sharply, and had been met with a curious gaze.

The painting, the artistry, was a thing of the past. He could never lift a brush, or spread his fingers again in the clay he used to breathe life into. It was time he faced it without mooning about the past. Without trying to jump back into it. It was gone.

Gentael Lifts Homespun Art to New Heights.

Hometown Boy Stuns with New Collection.

New York Galleries Are Interested.

Gentael Does Us Proud Again.

New Show Surprises and Gentael is Selling.

Then, the darker headlines, the ones he couldn't purge, no matter how hard he pushed himself to the limits of his physical endurance every day. The ones that still barged into his nightly dreams as if they had a right to. As if they had a life of their own, and were determined never to die. As if they would never leave, never go away.

Gentael show cancelled.

Hometown boy curiously absent at art show.

The most damning news piece of all was a buried two-line bit on page forty-five of the hometown rag, in between Old Ned selling firewood and an ad for used boats.

Gentael exits art scene. The Gazette *wishes him well in future endeavors.*

Ha. They'd made sure he wouldn't have any future endeavors in their damnable little town. Even though he'd brought so much attention to them that ever since, the art community there was bustling. Because of him, they'd had New York's attention for a while, though that had eventually dried up when no headliners emerged, but the community was still active, growing.

But him? He was gone.

No more dreams about being the artist he wanted to be. That part of his spirit had to be brought to heel. No matter how it surged at the most inopportune moments.

Determination seized him. Tomorrow, once they dealt with getting the kid settled, passing her over to the authorities—a pang sliced through him at that thought, but he pushed the feeling away—he'd clear the studio. He'd fucking torch it, if he had to.

All of it would be gone. Hell, he'd get Zach to build a bonfire in the yard and they'd do it together, once the kid and Og left. All the canvases, all the plans. The sketches, perspectives. His ideas. The binders.

All of it would be gone.

***

Nathan

Nathan turned again, trying to get comfortable, when what he really needed was to go to the damn bathroom. But Og still hadn't gone. Nathan had been listening so he could fucking go in peace, and not bump into him.

Nathan threw the thin cover off. His bladder was bursting. Muttering, he got up, padded out into the hallway from the darkness of his room into the ethereal, midnight-scape of the hallway, and bumped into something hard, warm, solid, and damn inviting.

"Hey, don't fall." Og reached out to steady him as Nathan jerked away. "You okay?"

The low tone. The newfound determination he'd had a mere moment ago evaporated. "I'm f-fine." Nathan could barely get the words out.

Og didn't drop his hand. If anything, his fingers tightened on Nathan's upper arm as if Og was the one in need of being steadied.

"Checked in on the kid," Og said. "She's snoring like a drunk sailor."

Nate raised his gaze and, bathed in the pale glow of moonlight, took in Og's intense stare. then Og shuttered his eyes and breathed the words, "Help me out here, buddy."

As if a strange, unseen force in his body was moving him, he leaned forward. He saw Og's eyes go wide, but the man didn't pull back. If anything, he steadied, and shifted forward. Nathan's lips met Og's and felt warmth and slight pressure. A swirling, low in his gut, an unbearable longing coursed through him as Og's grip tightened. His mouth opened, inviting Nathan in.

He was lost in a maze of feeling and want. This damn man was so real. So solid.

Og moved forward, then gently and steadily pushed Nathan against the wall.

God, he was so strong.

There was no question what was happening here. One more moment and—

"Noooo."

The screech sounded raw in the hallway and both men jumped. It echoed throughout the house, filled with fear. A door slammed downstairs, and they heard Zach yell, "Trasher? You okay? Guys? What's happening?" Nathan heard the banister's familiar creak as Zach grabbed it to catapult himself upstairs.

Og moved back. He was blinking rapidly, and Nate caught the uncertainty flowing from him, which was an odd and uncharacteristic reaction.

Nathan squared his shoulders, cleared his throat loudly, and called to Zach, "We're good. We're gonna check on her. Go back to bed."

Zach's voice floated up the staircase. "You sure?"

Nathan's hand was already on her porcelain doorknob. "Sure." He pushed the door open, and there was the young waif, sitting up in bed absolutely terrified.

***

Nathan

She looked so tiny in the huge space, it'd all but swallowed her. When they'd rushed to her side, her arms came up and she allowed them in turn to hug her.

Nathan hugged her softly, but with all his heart. Then Og had given her a huge bear hug.

Nathan wanted to yell at Og not to hurt her, but from the way she'd melted in his arms, he could see it was good for her to be held in massive tight arms.

"What happened, kid?" Og's voice was gentle.

No answer. Her expression was scattered, but nothing had happened. Perhaps it was the unfamiliarity of a new situation, or she had a bad dream. Despite the fact she'd clawed out a space for herself in shitty alleyways and god knew where else, including his stink-palace of a barn, as she'd called it, she was, at core, a scared little girl.

Og spoke to her with soft words. Words to comfort and give strength.

Then, after soothing words and ensuring she wasn't sick or anything that needed more immediate attention, he'd put her back to bed and tucked her in. A thought assailed Nathan as he stood a few minutes later at the bottom of the stairs, glass of milk for her in hand. From the little she'd said, and her age, he figured the worse of her life had happened at home.

Og was still in the room with Trasher. Apparently, she hadn't wanted them to leave her. After one look at his face, Og had announced he'd stay until she fell back to sleep. *All night if you need, kid,* he'd said. Nathan left Og sitting on a wooden chair beside her bed, holding her hand, talking to her soothingly, while the terror in her eyes dissipated with the steady kindness and attendance to her needs.

Zach met him, bundled in his oversize, navy velour robe. "She okay now?"

"She was pretty freaked. For all her balls and bravado, she's only a little kid."

"Is she gonna be okay? Will she get back to sleep?" His eyes widened. "Cookies. She'll need cookies." He turned, started down the hallway quickly.

"Wait. I hear something."

They both arched their necks toward the sound coming from behind the closed door upstairs. Og, with no kid's book around, no Harry Potter to read to her, had solved the problem. The dramatic low tones of his voice, followed by another, more high-pitched tone, were put together as if Og was reading her a delightful kid's story with multiple characters.

"What the hell is he reading?" Zach asked.

Nathan listened more carefully, then realized what it was, and he smiled. The paper that had been folded into the inside reaches of Og's jacket earlier, opened to the page he apparently perused daily to keep up with his business, his investments.

The man was reading her the *New York Times* financial pages.

Chapter Thirteen

Og

The little girl had fallen asleep, and Og hadn't met the handsome poet in the hallway again. The glimmer of the early morning sun was starting to paint the horizon. Og stood in the field, past the huge gray bulk of the barn, his gaze combing the white-tipped breakers in the cove. Cool winds rustled his makeshift pajamas. The crazy storm had blown over. Debris dotted the landscape.

He felt the pull of the surreal scene. God, these moments with nature drew him. Out here, away from all the noise and turmoil of the city, the fading moon leaving the sky as the sun got ready to make its appearance over the bay was a wonder. This little piece of land sticking out in the sea a marvel. The still dark seascape with the pale luminescence of morning on the horizon, teasing any fortunate onlooker with the dawn of a new day.

Instead of the peaceful calm the scene provided, it was anything but. His ear was glued to his cell, mired in an intense conversation with Jill, Palmer's admin, who had a habit of rising preternaturally early. She was more than his boss's right hand. She was Og's friend from a past life. He'd done her a favor long ago, and she'd never forgotten it.

Now they were deep in conversation. He'd snuck out of the house, careful not to wake the kid, the poet, or the bodyguard. He'd had a hell of a night.

Dealing with the kid. Lying on that mattress in an empty room having wet dreams. All of it tumultuous and too fucking emotional.

Nix on the poet. He couldn't get involved. He had too much on his plate. He had to find Michael and deal with whatever that held in store.

Jill said something that absolutely boiled his blood. He snorted loudly into the phone. "Are you fucking kidding me?"

"Og, listen to me. He's the boss."

He snarled his answer. "Fuck it."

"Yes, you can absolutely do that, if you want, but right now, Palmer is the man with the vacancy and the money. You want the job, and especially the money. Right?"

He gritted his teeth. "You know the answer."

"So, listen to me. Do what he says, even if you don't want to. Because if you don't...."

Because if I don't, Michael has no shot in hell.

"Fine. So what you're telling me is that I need to come up with a qualifying investment immediately. I can't wait for the charity thing I was counting on to open up. I have to make my decision now." Things pressed in on him even harder as the truth dawned. "Shit. I have to invest here, now."

For once, his always-in-control friend sputtered. "But you said it wasn't viable. That if Palmer looked in to it, he might not go for it, and if he doesn't, everything could go to hell, only a bit later."

Jill's voice was suddenly quiet, and he sensed the heartbreak in it because damnit, she cared about him. She knew why he needed Palmer's job so bad.

Why the hell had the family trust been made into a charitable trust? The last joke his family had played on him. If only it had been a normal trust, they could've gotten their hands on the money somehow and Michael would be safe right now.

He'd accepted the fact that it was a charitable trust, and that the mechanics of it would benefit him only in years hence. It had been tough, as a young man, to see all that money there, and know he wouldn't have any of it until he was practically too old to care, but he'd made his peace with that. He told himself it would make him tough, more ambitious and self-reliant. And it had. He'd done well enough, and no access to easy money had played into it. When the problems with Michael had surfaced, Og'd had to get on with the job to save his brother, once again.

"You have to come up with a viable investment immediately, or he won't even look at your CV."

The awful truth reverberated deep in his gut. He'd known he had to get away from this weirdly utopian spot, and do it fast, but circumstances required him to chain himself to it even tighter.

"It'll have to become viable. The most brilliant investment possible. It'll have to become that overnight."

***

Og

Og had hiked down the lane out onto the road, went to the 'Stang and drove her back. The road still wasn't cleared, but soon enough it would be.

He went back inside, waited in the kitchen, had a cup of joe, and strategized.

Two hours later, the rest of the house came to life, and a messy, haphazard type of happiness reigned in the old kitchen. Trasher stumbled down the stairs, hair tousled from sleep, and planted herself, eyes diverted, into the wooden chair she'd sat in the night before.

Her eyes didn't stay downcast for long. Zach plunked a hot bowl of oatmeal in front of her and watched for her reaction. When he got it—along the lines of *what's this horrible, world-ending bowl of goop*—he smiled, as if the universe was right again.

A noisy argument ensued, but surprisingly, it didn't take long. Both parties seemed to have surreptitiously figured out each other's weaknesses and strengths. The deal was struck and made. One steaming bowl of steel-cut oatmeal without sugar equaled as many stacks of pancakes as the young negotiator could eat in a forty-five-minute window, after the oatmeal was consumed.

Clearly, the little girl had her bluster back. In fact, if Og wasn't mistaken, that was the whole purpose of the scene. Zach wasn't stupid. Bodyguard, in more ways than one.

The man who had thrown Og's stomach into such a pile of knots was nowhere to be found. Those clandestine few moments in the hallway had clinched it: he had to hightail it away from the little pastoral peninsula as fast as he could.

Part of him told himself it was no biggie. Guys were attracted to each other all the time. So, he really didn't know why there was a big ball of something leaden in his throat. Hell. It was probably that he was out of his training routine. A few days at the gym, back in NY, and he'd be fine.

Until poet-god appeared in the doorway.

Preoccupied, that tanned face softened for a second when his gaze lit on Trasher. The beginnings of a smile flashed, then stayed. The guy had a soft spot for the kid, despite the trouble she'd caused. He'd be such a good dad.

Then poet-god strolled to the kitchen counter, switched on the burner under the old tin can of a kettle.

"Your coffee's pressed." Zach's tone was soft.

"Really?"

"Yeah. Heard you moving around. Knew you'd be down."

Nathan turned, and Og found himself unavoidably in the poet's sightline. Nathan gave him a brisk nod, so momentary it was almost as if he hadn't seen it.

A deep flash of irritation hit him. It bugged him. No one overlooked him. No one. He'd see how Nathan would ignore him after he made his investor pitch.

Nathan poured coffee into his mug, then took a big gulp. "Someone's coming to see the room today."

Zach turned from putting away tea towels into a drawer, still finishing up more unpacking. "That was fast. I posted it last night."

"Well, he's coming today. Needs a place, and the rent seems to be no issue."

"Let's hope he's not pulling your leg. Remember, we've got something else important to get settled today."

Nathan raised a brow.

Zach's gaze tracked over Trasher's head, then dipped.

"Me. The inconvenient child," she said between mouthfuls. All three men took a double take and stared at Trasher, who was now in mid-slurp. She heaved the last huge spoonful of soppy oatmeal into her mouth, swallowed, then eyed the stack of apple pancakes. "You gotta get me gone."

Pain filtered through Og's system. The poet and the bodyguard looked sick, too. He had to take this in hand. "It's for your own good, kid. You can't be living with three men."

Nathan and Zach both turned abruptly toward him and said in unison. "Three?"

Zach gave him a suspicious look. "The renter may not take the room."

Og answered quickly, impatient. "I didn't mean the renter. Hell, that would make it four men."

Shit. He didn't mean to tip his hand this soon. He braced his body, angled forward, and stared at the three of them. "Yeah. I meant three. You, you, and me. You know this is a losing proposition out here. You'll never get an investor, probably tried and no one bit. I've made my decision. You toe the line, we do things my way, and I'm in. When I say I'm in, I'm here on-site, full-time. As in live-in. No rent, either."

"Live here?" Nathan's expression was positively horrified. "With us?"

"That's what living here typically means. This place has got to be whipped into shape. I don't see anyone else mixing mortar."

"But your home. Wherever you live now. Can you leave it?"

He'd divested everything he owned to free up money to get Michael back home. Even the 'Stang had been on the block, but wasn't worth enough and he needed a vehicle. He wasn't going to tell him all that, though. "Not your concern. That's the condition. I'm here, full-time, without any complaint, and you get all the money you need. If not, then nothing doing. You choose."

Chapter Fourteen

Nathan

Og wasn't leaving. An incredible sense of relief unfurled in Nathan's belly at the same time a tension ratcheted across the front of his chest.

The full import of Og's words hit him. *You do things my way.* This was Nathan's dream, not the damn boxer's. Nathan's jaw tightened, and he snarled, "Outside."

"Huh?"

Nathan didn't answer. He headed for the back door, grabbed something off the counter, then plowed onward, the brittle wood slapping the misshapen frame behind him.

You've caught it now, bud, he heard Zach say.

Nathan stood there, his breath coming fast as the sun bathed the scene of after-storm carnage in a warm glow. He was ready to absolutely rip out the bloody heart of the man who was messing with his dream.

The back door slammed again and Og faced him down, and the word emanated from him like a pistol shot. "Speak." Every muscle in Og's frame was tense. His fingers weren't curled into a fist, but they were rigid.

Nathan didn't care.

"You're on my turf. In my home. Whether or not it continues to be my home, that's my shit. My shit, and mine alone. In my home, it's done my way."

Og's answer was a steely gaze.

Nathan continued. "My dream. My mission. It'll work out my way or it will fall into the biggest disaster of my whole fucking life. But it will be mine."

If he thought Og was going to back down, he got the answer. Fast. "Nice speech," Og drawled, leaning on the wall as if he didn't have a care in the world. "But so we're clear. I'm offering you the money you need to get this place ready for whatever cockamamie dream you've got. I'm giving you terms that would make grown men cry. We'll get this place fixed up then you can carry on with your plans."

Og's gaze shifted, and Nathan realized he wasn't looking at him anymore, but far away. Over to where the dirt met the sand, then farther out until he was staring at the waves. As if memorizing them in that split second, watching them hold for a brief flash of eternity, then break and form new configurations, new translucent lines.

Og turned back to him and continued. "It's all got to be done in one month. Then I'll be out of your hair, and you can play innkeeper to the brokenhearted and messed up, whatever the fuck you want. If you say no, you and I both know you can screw your mission in the fucking ass and you'll never see it again."

Nate watched as Og's gaze hardened, even while the waves danced in the distance.

"Your choice."

***

Og

Og had seen the type before. It would take barely a New York minute and the guy would crumple. They all showed big bravado, but when pushed, they caved. It almost made the man a bit less attractive, and he was sorry for that. It would burst his dream, mess with the attraction, but Og knew how to get what he wanted, and this time, the stakes were too high. He'd even mess with poet-dude.

Nathan's gaze met his, and he watched for the cave, but it didn't come.

Wordlessly, Nathan pulled something up deep from his pants pocket and deposited it into Og's palm. The 'Stang's keys. "See ya."

The man turned, stalked back into the old house, and the door slammed behind him.

Five minutes later, Zach pushed the door open and sat beside him as Og sat on the old, gray weathered bin outside. "Let's not pretend anymore."

"None of that was pretend in there. Or out here. I'm willing to invest if—"

"Yeah, yeah. Two dicks, pissing contest. Got all that, and so did the child, through the window. It wasn't closed, professor. You overplayed your hand. Horribly."

Og shrugged. It hid his surprise, he hoped. He hadn't expected poet-boy to have a backbone. "If he won't—"

"Don't play games with him or me. I'm here to tell you, you miscalculated. If you want any chance in hell of getting close to him, of getting in his pants…"

He shot Zach a sharp glance but Zach snorted, unimpressed. "It doesn't take a research scientist to feel the sparks. I'd need a heat suit to miss all that. Even the child knows. Listen, getting this place right is serious to him. His plans, his life's work. He's not only in it to feel good for a moment, or a week, or a month. This is a life mission, and at the moment, you've pushed him as far as he'll go."

Og stared deep into Zach's eyes, and met understanding. It may have been deep, buried, but it was there. Buried out of concern for his best friend. The man really loved Nathan, would go to the wall for him.

"Okay, fine. Say you're right. I messed up. What do I need to do to get him on board?" He added hastily, "It benefits him too, and this dream thing he's got going."

Zach's gaze came down in intensity. "Not sure what's in it for you, but that'll become obvious in the long run. I fully believe that. In the meantime, tone it down. Be his friend. He's not the one-night-stand type. He's got a thing for you. I can feel it. He doesn't love easily. He's been too hurt."

Og's curiosity was piqued. "What happened?"

"That'll be for him to tell you. If you can't really care for him, get to know him and decide you can love him, take those keys and get on your way and don't ever come back. Got it?"

Og blinked. Love him? There was heat, for sure. Heat led to fusing, to release. Closeness, in the moment. Then he'd be gone. Og did not do love.

"So?" Zach asked the question Og was asking himself.

He'd keep those thoughts to himself. Now, the game was the deal, and he had to play harder than he'd ever had to before. Because of Michael. "What do I do now?"

"You might start with finding out about his father and his past. Ease up on all the macho stuff. Let him know he's got a voice, that you'll work with him. You can still hold the purse-strings. Heaven knows they're yours. Without easing up, that's all you'll have."

***

Trasher

Holy fried amazeballs. She could see them from her position behind the chest in the front vestibule. Her back ached as she forced herself low, but at least she had a bead on them. They were both uptight. When boxer dude came and talked at softie, she saw the tension in both of them, like they were ready to blow.

Blood. Soon there would be blood on the floor, on the wall. And she'd be told to wash it off when they were done, when one was broken and the other glad, with a weird kind of ferocity. The water in the old pail, as she scrubbed with the worn towel, would turn pale pink, the red wafting through the water. Mixing with it. Then it would all turn sickly pink, then red. Bright red.

She'd retch and vomit. They'd slap her, and she'd be forced to continue.

All the blood....

She heard a voice raise, saw softie protest. She saw their bodies tense, the way they avoided looking at each other, so much so she wanted to scream. She was tired, so damn tired of screaming.

Then boxer leaned closer to softie and she shuddered. Softie tightened more. Pulled back. Her heart raced, pounding so hard it filled her whole chest until there was nothing else there, only the ferocious thuds.

She so wished she was a princess with all her heart. One who could snap her fingers and change the world. Make people get along. Stop being mean. But that wasn't for her, and never would be. Pain cracked into the pounding, swirled into an awful mix of bad, and getting worse.

She held her breath.

Miracle of miracles, boxer man pulled back. Softie relaxed. Their voices went low, quiet. The tension dipped, and drained.

Then boxer man—holy hell, she liked him—put his hand out, offering it to softie. Softie—and oh, she liked him so much, too—looked long and hard at boxer man's face then at his outstretched hand.

Take it, take it, take it.

He did. He took it. They were getting along. Softie held it longer than she expected, and a moment passed between them. They shook those clasped hands, broke apart. Smiled.

It was like the sun broke out in her little world. Like it was a day with rumpled bedcovers, with steaming muffins for breakfast that Mom had made. When Dad laughed and hid them in the bedside table drawer to tease Mom, and they played together, her jumping on the bed, getting into a pillow fight with Dad and Adam. Then Dad hauled them out and they ate them all together in bed before falling back to sleep. Mom forgetting the dishes as she lay back on the pillow, breathing deeply. Dad would later sneak off to wash them off, then come back and join them until they all woke up in a tangle, lazy. Together.

No worries. No trouble. Play and fun and sunshine.

Play and fun and good times until the trouble came.

It always did, growing ever fiercer.

She shrank back from her hiding place by the door, determined. She was going to watch for the first sign of the trouble. When it came, she'd be on her way, to whatever horror her life took her to.

Again.

***

Nathan

Og positioned the wheelbarrow into place in front of Nathan as they worked together in the yard. The details of the deal had been worked out and agreed upon. For a short while, they were stuck together like glue. Then they'd gotten to work in the endeavor of getting the house and property into shape. The yard was already showing the evidence of their care.

"How are you at creating a work plan?"

Nathan rolled his eyes. He grabbed another log that had been stacked by the back of the house and threw it into the wheelbarrow. "I may have a slight acquaintance with the concept." He grunted, this time picking up two logs and tossing them. They flew together in unison and hit the top of the pile, bits of bark flying every which way.

Og stopped, put his hands on his waist, and gave him a solid look. "Is that your way of telling me I'm slightly brain-dead?"

Nathan's lips curled in a smirk. "Slightly?"

"Fine. We'll put together a work plan after lunch. By the way, was that a quiche Zach was putting together a few minutes ago with homemade crust?"

"Possibly. We have a lot of it, because as you know…"

Og grinned. "Yeah, yeah. Real men do eat quiche." This time the smirk transitioned into a full-blown smile.

Nathan scanned Og as the man turned, picked up the shovel again, and dug at the oddly placed trunk in the center of the yard. This cleaning-up-the-yard session, working to make it presentable for would-be renters, was proceeding well. Not the least of it was the eye candy he had staring him in the face whenever he looked in Og's direction. Right now, he couldn't have asked for a better sight.

The pale T-shirt Zach had loaned Og stretched across his pecs, splotches of sandy dirt on it. It was a bit threadbare, and there were a few holes where tanned skin showed through. He'd declined a work jacket, said he'd be hot, especially when he was working up a sweat.

And, oh yeah…he was.

Nathan could see himself licking up and down those pecs. Tasting them through the myriad of tiny holes, then diving under. Sampling Og's wares. All that skin. Then proceeding south, to that prominent bulge that kept catching Nate's attention.

Hey. Og had said he had amazing balls. Nothing like finding out for himself.

Ogling aside, none of this meant Nate didn't have worries. If he wanted to avoid questions and get rid of all of the mementos of the past, he had to clear out the studio. It would be a little harder with Og underfoot, but Nate needed to do it. Burn everything. He'd find a way to do it when Og wasn't around.

For right now, though, the man was definitely around.

It took all Nate had in him to not run, wrap his arms around Og from behind. Squeeze. Hard. Of course, once he did that, he'd stroke his fingers all the way down to—

"Freakin' manual labor."

The words speared into his brain and suddenly the impish face of Trasher appeared in front of him. His face reddened. Had he been gawking? He tried to hide it by sputtering, "Huh?"

"This is so not fair. I'm being conscripted into manual labor." She glared at him. "There are laws, you know."

"What the heck are you talking about?"

"I'm to pick green crap." Her eyes narrowed. "Parsley or eggplant or sage or something disgusting"

"Well, eggplant's purple and not in season, and neither is parsley, so I'm guessing a bit of new growth sage."

Trasher frowned and bent, examined some of the weeds in the untidy little garden under the kitchen window. "Whatever."

Nathan smiled. "You added eggplant, didn't you?"

She gave him the side eye, but under the surreptitious exterior and the face that still sported a bit of dried jam on one cheek, he thought he saw a grin struggling to break out. "You don't question an actress about her method," she challenged.

God, he loved this little girl. How, in one short day....

"I'm waiting."

He couldn't help himself. It wasn't what she'd meant, but that didn't matter. He took two big steps over to her, and as she straightened with a suspicious look on her face and leaned away from him, he squatted beside her, pulled her close to him, circled his arms around her, and folded her into a great big hug.

He felt her frame quiver, and he started to release her in case she was scared, but then—she simply melted into his arms. Let go entirely. At that point nothing could have dragged him away.

"Guys?" Og's voice reached his ears. "What's going on? Everything okay?"

Ever the protector.

She always seemed to give hugs with her fists curled into little balls, not open palm. He didn't know what it meant, but he was sure she had a reason. When those little fists came around him and he felt them thunk on his back, while her arms tightened, nothing had felt so good in a long time.

It about burst his heart.

Then something insistent, cold and warm at the same time, pushed at them. He opened his eyes quickly and there she was. Bright-eyed and literally bushy-tailed, with tail wagging.

"Molly," Trasher screamed in delight. "She's come back."

He whispered the words in her ear, wishing it could be true. Wanting it to be true, not traitorous. Because she may not be there that long, and he knew that, but it needed saying. She needed to know the truth of this one thing at least. "She'll always come back when you're around, honey. She loves to play with you." He paused, projecting his feelings onto the dog. "She loves you so much."

Trasher rolled her head, looked him in the eyes for a quick flash, then buried her face in his shoulder again. Her one hand was on the dog's muzzle, and it was pushing into that small palm. She hugged him harder, if that was possible.

"Nathan. There's someone on the phone to talk to you." Zach's voice floated out through the kitchen window. "A Missus Merriwether."

The blow struck even while he held the little girl in his arms. His heart spasmed. The woman he'd been told was going to call soon to make arrangements and was going to take this little girl, this precious little street rat/urchin/cherub, away from them was on the phone.

Waiting to talk to him about taking Trasher away.

***

Og

Og's throat tightened as he watched the scene. Silly poet-man, the sweet little girl who had no one, and the insanely happy mutt who made the rounds and couldn't seem to stay away from them. From any of them.

He took a look around the old house and its yard. Definitely a dilapidated homestead, but the emotions that were bursting from it were huge. He looked up at the mottled yellow-brownish brick, the cracks here and there. The stalwart chimney that created the highest point, the oddly shaped trees that surrounded it. Scrappy somehow, yet he noticed they ringed it tightly, as if protecting it. The silly pig emblem on top, and the cherub. He wondered how he'd ended up on this special spot.

If only he and Michael had had a place like this. Full of love, spirit. Hope.

Og had to stop playing silly little dream games, playing house in his head. He had to get on with his task.

Everything changed, though, as he watched the girl and the sweet poet. Darkness fell across the scene as Zach yelled out about the call. He saw Nathan abruptly release the young girl, then stumble into the house with pain in his frame. He saw her bewilderment, and the moment she caught on something had changed, horribly. Two seconds later, there was spilled sage on the ground, and she was gone. Running toward the barn with the confused animal yipping, running after her. She fled toward the old building and yanked the door open.

The black hole swallowed them both up.

Where love, acceptance, and joy had been only two seconds earlier, there was now nothing. Emptiness. The sense of something missing remained, but soon everything settled, and it was like what had played out in front of him had never existed.

The gargoyles leered from that long-forgotten scene, and he shivered.

You can never get away, no matter what you do. You can never get back what you lost.

The breeze turned cold as he picked up the shovel, winced at the momentary pain in his hand, adjusted, then started his task once again.

Digging.

Chapter Fifteen

Nathan

The appointment was set. Mrs. Merriwether, the woman from the agency, was coming tomorrow to take Trasher away.

Nathan's eyes were closed as he sat at the kitchen table, defeated. He'd told Zach to give him time alone. Zach had set off to the neighbors to borrow a pie plate or something. Some crazy nonsense that didn't matter anymore. The bowl of whipped eggs sat on the counter, the little piles of ham, onion, and green pepper tidily diced on the wooden cutting board. Drying out. So much for the quiche.

The little girl. Wasn't it Nate's mandate to take care of the brokenhearted?

What a fraud he was.

At least he'd had pleasure and joy in his family life, but the darkness in Trasher's past life that Mrs. Merriwether had hinted at had shocked him even though he'd told himself to be ready for anything.

They'd identified Trasher from the scant papers Nathan had found in the barn among her things. And if it was a correct ID, her history was awful. Her parents had died, gone missing in one of the horrible storms in this part of the country, and they'd never been found.

The worst part of it was the foster home she'd been put in. A couple gaming the system, they'd left her with friends who were drug addicts, and when the drugs ran out, as they did regularly, there was violence. Luckily, most of it hadn't been against her, but she'd had to watch far too much of it. Live with the threats of it coming for her.

What a life she'd had. How different from his own. Nate had been blessed with such a good home life, with parents who cared. When he'd realized as a little kid that some lived with terror every day, he'd clutched his stomach, felt such pain. There were some horrors too large for a small boy's brain to comprehend. He'd also realized his sensitivity had a life of its own.

Thank god he'd had parents who loved him. Words of affection, humor, empathy, and kindness. Despite his having been diagnosed at an early age with learning disabilities, his parents had always had one thousand percent faith in him and in his abilities. That had been the daily facts of his life. He couldn't remember more than one or two occasions when his dad had ever been mad or short with him.

He knew he had been blessed with the best family life, with the best parents in the world, and in thanks, he'd torn their lives apart.

Now, when he really wanted to, he wasn't being given a chance to rewrite history. To help the little girl who'd already burrowed her way into his soul. He'd spoken to the woman, poured out his heart. She'd taken the references he offered, but told him he'd have to become a registered foster care giver before they would allow Trasher to stay with him. That process would take months, and who knew what would happen to her in the meantime.

He'd kept the secret of trying to keep Trasher from Zach and Og. It had been a wild jump into fantasy. Something that would heal his and Trasher's troubled hearts.

He felt the gentle pressure of a hand on his shoulder. His eyes flew open and he jerked his head up. Og. "Oh. It's you."

"She ran into the barn, and I've given her a few moments. Lord knows what she's doing."

"Probably letting her heart break." The words escaped his lips, harsh.

Og pulled out the chair beside him, sat down and leaned forward. "You have no choice."

Nathan set his mouth and didn't answer.

Og's hand settled over his own. The kindness of the simple gesture touched him. But it didn't take away the pain.

"I know you feel like crap."

Nathan shrugged. "Like hell."

"And why are you taking all this upon yourself?"

He spat the word out, "Because."

Because I'm supposed to take care of people. I can create the means. I can. And most of all because I damn well know how they feel.

But none of those words came out of his mouth because he simply couldn't. Didn't have the energy. He was too miserable.

His eyes still closed, he felt a hand under his chin, tilting it up gently. Fingers brushed his cheek tenderly, lingering, almost uncertain in their welcome. Then a warm pressure from a hand holding his jaw, cradling it. Then lips touched his, feather soft.

The halt in his own breath, the answering one in Og's.

An ache spread, spiked. Og nipped lightly at his bottom lip, but suddenly, Nathan was impatient. He parted his lips, opened to the man and invited him in as desire enveloped him. Passion pitched deep and hard as Og's tongue traced the seam of his mouth, then dipped in, kissing him, without holding back.

A world in that kiss. Want, undercurrents of everything he'd ever felt deep in his soul, bursting free, seeking release. Electricity surged in him at Og's exhaled moan. The man's hand curled around the nape of his neck, pulling him closer, and his own shaking hands rose, and gripped strong biceps.

The pleasure rocked his chest and core as Og moved closer to him. Pain snarled in him too, because he wanted it to go further. Right now. Yesterday. Forever.

He'd fought it, but ever since Og had entered Nate's life with a cocky attitude, strength, and the promise of protection, he'd been helpless to fight the man.

Og stopped and rested his forehead against Nathan's. "Trasher."

Guilt roiled in him. How had he allowed himself to forget, even only in that one split second? These momentary flashes of joy, of abandon, but with her crying her guts out in the barn alone, he felt like shit.

"Oh god. She needs me. Us."

A finger pressed on his lips. "Don't start. There's nothing wrong here. We're going to take care of her. In a couple of minutes, as soon as we collect ourselves."

Of course, Og was right, though the stab of shame rippled through him. "Okay. Hell."

Worse was thinking about what she must have been through already in her young life. "She kept saying the word 'blood' through the night last night, sleep-talking, and scared. I almost shook her awake, to get those damn words out of her mouth." He flinched at the recollection. "Then she settled, so I let her be."

"You did the right thing."

However, the pain was collecting, and he so badly wanted to flush it away. "Why do you think she picked that stupid name?"

"Trasher? I don't know. Maybe she needed something to divert us, saw the garbage around her. Or maybe someone called her trash when she was younger and she adopted it out of defiance. If she picked the name on purpose, that rings of power. Even at her young age"

"When she was younger?" Nathan snorted in disgust. "She's a small child."

Og sighed. "Young, and yet miles older than she should be. I want to rip all that garbage from her soul."

Nathan decided to tell the truth, no matter if he had the man's sudden scorn for his weakness. It wouldn't be the first time he was told he was too sensitive. "I wish she didn't have to go."

Og squeezed his hand, not an inkling of recrimination in his expression. "They'll take good care of her. You would've ended up in trouble with the law if you hadn't reported her. You can't simply take a young kid, pull her out of the world and plant her in yours, much as you'd like to."

Nathan was starting to collect himself. "It's all so fucked up. She's been running from something, something bad. I can tell the way she looks sometimes that she's remembering. Here, she could have some peace. Nobody would hurt her. Ever. I'd make sure of it."

"If we did it legal, then yeah. It takes a while to get certified to be a foster parent. I know that much."

Nathan shook his head. "Sucks."

"When are they coming?"

"Tomorrow. Eleven."

Og squeezed his hand one more time, then rose. "Well, it's on us now to make the transition the happiest one possible." He cut a stalwart, strong figure. "The work plan can wait. So can the chores. The three of us promised her the biggest cheeseburger known to mankind for the taking. I suggest we go, find the best place possible, and make sure that little girl has the happiest meal she's ever had, with the most attention she'll ever get from three awesome men. Whataya say?"

"What the hell are we waiting for?"

***

Og

They walked into the musty darkness. Through hay and debris strewn on the ancient wood planks, through dust moats dancing in thin rays of sunlight. They found her where they knew, all too well, she'd be: in the old horse stall, Molly pressed up beside her, the cream fur on the canine's neck wet with the child's tears.

When she'd needed comfort, she'd fled to the place where the spirit of horses still danced in the air.

Molly lifted plaintive eyes to them as they approached. *Help her.*

"Trasher, honey," Og crooned. Nathan went to the other side and put his arm over her heaving frame. She cried all the harder.

"We don't want you to go," Nathan cooed.

Nathan spoke the truth. Not merely for himself, but for all of them. Og wished he could stay and be part of the little girl's life with this sensitive man. Crazy thoughts, surely brought forth by emotions for a helpless child.

Her words escaped through sobs, "Then w-why… do I have to?"

Og squatted in front of them. Someone had to take the situation in hand. Emotion wound through the air, too thick. "The people who are coming will take good care of you. This is what they do." He swallowed hard. "They take care of little kids and match them with good families." The explanation came out shaky. He tried to find something positive to say. "You're a terrific kid. They'll find you an amazing mom and dad."

He felt like bawling. Words he hadn't planned blurted from him. "We love you."

That didn't have the desired effect. She sobbed, and her mutterings came out super soft this time. He strained to hear. "Then why are you doing this to me?"

A look passed between them, intense. Og nodded. "It's the law. We don't have any choice, honey."

The features on her face unclenched, though her eyes stayed closed. She seemed to tilt her head toward them. "You mean, if you had a choice you would?"

"Oh, honey," Nathan exclaimed. "If we had a choice, you'd stay. Forever and ever. You know we need a sergeant in the kitchen to keep us all in line. Manor House needs you."

Her face softened. "Zach too?"

Nathan's hand rubbed her shoulder, his voice thick. "Especially Zach. He's nuts about you, honey."

She finally peeked her eyes open, trained her gaze on Og. How she figured out there was a question there, he'd never know. Kid was insightful. Smart. "You too?"

"Me too, little one."

**

Og

The tears dried. Zach had given his own batch of hugs, and he'd expressed his devotion to her as well.

They'd then presented a bright picture of the future to her, though she hadn't quite bought that yet. However, when they'd told her about the special lunch and that they'd actually called and made reservations for Miss Trasher and her three gentlemen, all was well, for the moment. It was probably the first time she'd lived in the glow of love from a group of people, all focused on her.

"Snazzy ride," Trasher said as she skipped to the car and started to climb in the backseat. Zach had hand-washed her clothes the night before, leaving her looking almost presentable.

"Shut up, kid, and don't get peanut butter on the seats. Those are pure Italian leather." Og slid into the driver seat and put the key in the ignition.

"This crap?"

He smiled. "Well, they will be, in the next heap I own."

"Nathan, did you bring my peanut butter?"

Nathan laughed and Og smiled. It was crazy how happy that kid made him. Nathan had his hand on the door handle when a lone figure approached them from the side. The man's suit jacket looked out of place, but the jeans and T-shirt he wore underneath fit right in, and the closely cropped beard that covered the lower half of his face didn't make him too hard to look at. He glanced at the car and the group of them leaving.

"Uh, hello. Is this where the room for rent is?"

Nathan blinked, then rallied. "Yes. Yes, it is. But...." He stuttered, then made a decision. "Something really important's come up. I'm sorry, but we can't meet with you right now. We're not available."

"Oh." The guy seemed taken aback. "But there is a room for rent?"

Nathan snorted. "More than one. Only one in really good repair right now, but the others are livable, if necessary." He waved his hand at the mess in the yard, the tattered plastic they'd torn off the tiny cottage's windows and doors then shoved in a wooden barrel so the wind wouldn't grab it. "We're in the process of turning it all into decent housing."

"And that bit?" The stranger inclined his head toward the tiny cottage.

"That's the cottage. It won't be ready for months. It's been in disrepair for years. I wish it was done already, but it's not. Hey, we would've loved to show you, but if you're in a hurry... sorry. Other priorities." He turned, let his gaze rest on Trasher a moment, then pivoted back to the man. "Sorry to waste your time."

"No worries. I understand." The man went off in the direction of the road, and Nathan climbed into the car, beside Og.

Og turned and searched his face. Nathan had made a decision to lose out on a potential renter, and he needed the dough. Desperately. Nathan craned his neck around, fastened his gaze on Trasher again, and the look that came over his face was filled with joy. Complete, bottomless joy.

And deep in Og's gut, the moment freeze-framed. He knew that no matter what happened, no matter where life took him, he'd always remember the look on Nathan's face as he got ready to treat the little girl he loved to a meal she'd never forget. When that man sacrificed a pile of money he needed merely to keep a promise to her, maybe it wasn't smart, but it was heartfelt.

"Now, little lady. Ready for your eat-a-thon?" Nathan grinned.

"Um, think I'm ready," she sassed. "I've been waiting, like forever."

"Well, wait no longer." Nathan turned back to the front, buckled up.

Tucked in to one of the wooden booths at Refuge Bay's answer to a famous burger franchise, waiting for her "Haha" meal, Trasher was excited. The rustic little diner attached to the side of the gas station was named McDoodles and was run by Sandy and Gary Duncan. A sign above the diner was emblazoned with a picture of a golden three-posted fence, stating: "Five Hundred Eighty-Two Proudly Served."

With the sights, sizzles, and scents of a classic diner all around them, Trasher's feet were kicking at the wooden center post of the table.

"You might want to tone that racket down," Nathan suggested. She'd squealed in delight when they'd walked in and she was asked about her special reservation, momentarily forgetting her need to maintain the façade of seven-year-old superiority. Now he was on her about her manners, and rightfully so.

"It's my party. I get to do whatever I want." She jutted her chin out, but Og noted the kicking died down pretty quickly.

A bushy-eyebrowed old man wearing an apron approached them. Seeing as Sandy the waitress had taken their order, this was a surprise, not to mention the frilly white apron over his shirt, pants, and lime-green suspenders looked ridiculous. "You the kid who's going to eat her face off?"

Trasher focused in on him, and her grip on Zach's hand tightened. She didn't answer.

"She's the one," Og answered for her.

"Just checking to see if you want to add anything else to that order."

"We may actually add a batch of onion rings," Nathan requested. "Can you do a big communal basket?"

"You pay, we do," the old man said. "I'll make sure of it. By the way, name's Emmett. You need anything that's off-menu, holler for me. Anything to flip the cook off." He winked at Trasher as he left.

"What are you looking forward to the most, princess? The crazy huge burger with the extra bacon—the Big Moo—the barrel full of fries, the Big Bay Milkshake, or the Gull Gull Apple Pie?" Nathan looked as excited as the kid.

"Princess *Trasher*, you mean."

Nathan's eyes widened as he said, "As you wish."

The kid stopped for a moment, blinked, then continued on as if nothing had happened. But Og had seen it. *The Princess Bride* moment. The shock that someone would do something for her. Cater to her, and let the world know that they would, because she was important.

The phone rang, and Og saw it was the call he was expecting. Jill. He excused himself and quickly stepped outside.

All this work—the deal, the labor around Manor House—none of it meant anything unless Palmer bit.

Jill had good news. The "charity" had been approved, and he was in. Relief swept through him.

Now. The most important call to make. He tossed a glance back inside, saw the quick look of hero worship Trasher gave Nathan and Zach. Hell. If she could *stay* with them—and at that thought something in his chest seized up—she'd do anything for them. True love was like that.

You took care of those you loved, paid the cost. Always.

Michael had done it with him. It had been hero worship, a sweet puppy love, and that had been Og's undoing. Michael had wanted to prove he was tough like his brother. Og had been clueless, didn't see the path the kid was taking. Because of him, Michael was in a South American jungle, held prisoner, a hostage taken by hostile forces.

The Watcher was keeping eyes on him. He'd have told Og if Michael had been killed, then would move on to his next critical case.

Alive, but suffering.

Og took an inventory of his accomplishments over the last few days. The little girl inside was happy at the moment. The deal with Nathan had been brokered, more or less, decently. The most important part of the operation was waiting. Og straightened as his resolve strengthened, became steel.

The one promise he'd made to his brother over and over in their short time together blazed through his mind. When the kid had been scared, when he'd had nightmares because of the countless foster homes he'd been in before they'd found their way back to each other, Og had promised one thing: *No matter where you end up, buddy, no matter who's got you or where you are, I'll come for you. Always.*

Michael had clung to his arm, fear piercing his expression. He'd asked in that tiny voice, "But what if you can't find me? What if someone takes me away again?" The kid hadn't been making stuff up. It'd happened. He knew it was a real threat.

Og always replied the same way, and he'd meant it. "They can never take you far enough away, kid. I'll come for you. Always."

There was only one thing left to do. He punched in the number. Once the Watcher answered, the accelerated search for Michael was on.

No matter what it cost financially or to Og's life.

***

Nathan

Nathan glanced around the small restaurant. It was a bit "down home" for such a momentous occasion in a little girl's life, but he knew the power of such occasions. Of memories.

Underneath all the emotion, he wanted to craft something that would stay with her no matter where life took her.

It may have been only a tiny diner on a backward little peninsula sticking out into the Atlantic, but he wanted her to feel enveloped in love. To be the center point of joy, to feel the attention, the abundance. He wanted her to always remember that one time she'd had three men doting on her, making sure she got whatever she wanted or needed.

The way she was cuddling closer to Zach, as if she'd been there all her life, and the looks she threw up at Og, bordering on delight interspersed with hero worship, *and* the snappy comments she came up with that they all howled at did good things for Nate's heart.

He couldn't overlook one other thing. Og being there with them made it all feel right. Stable. Somehow, in a matter of days, Og was already an integral part of Nathan's life. It may be foolish, may not make sense, but there it was. He closed his eyes for a moment, and when he opened them, Og's gaze was on him. Smiling.

His heart beat roughly, and he smiled back.

Their order finally arrived.

Sandy, with her father-in-law in tow carrying more plates, appeared at their table. Cheerful glances from the tables around them added to the feeling of celebration.

"Here you go, missy." Sandy laid the centerpiece of the order before Trasher. A huge, oversized homemade burger, still practically sizzling on a homemade bun. Ketchup dripped off one side, expertly fried bacon crackling on the top, all smothered with organic farm cheddar.

The way that kid's eyes widened was a crime.

"And here's the really good stuff." Emmett reached around his daughter-in-law, actually pushing her out of the way in his eagerness. She jumped back a couple of steps, shooting Trasher a grin and a wink, obviously not minding.

He put an obscenely huge basket of extra well-done fries in the center of the table, along with another of crisply fried onion rings. "Figured you needed a communal basket of the taters too." He looked at Trasher for approval. Upon receiving it, he bent low to her and stage-whispered, "Nothing like eating all together from one big heap, is there, honey?"

He straightened, looked at his daughter-in-law, then announced, "Fries are bottomless." Sandy's eyebrows winged up high in feigned surprise, but he looked at her as he repeated, "Bottomless. Fries are bottomless." He turned his attention to Trasher. "Don't forget, little one."

Trasher found her voice. "Who you calling little one?"

He sputtered, put on a little dramatic act of shock. Clutched at his heart. Then said, "Pardon me, *mademoiselle*. Your name would be?"

She smiled, tilted her head. "Princess Trache'."

"*Ah oui, madame. En Francais?*"

"*Oui,*" she added, with the sweetest little flick of her head, participating in the play without missing a beat. Her oddly cut hair bounced, and in that moment, Nathan knew he'd never forget her. Ever.

"Well, y'all dig in," Sandy said, hooking her arm into her father-in-law's and tugging on him. "I gotta get the boss back to command central. They'll fall apart without him. Plus," she added, with a meaningful side-eye to the old man, "we need to get working on more of those bottomless, hand-cut fries, which you just added to the menu."

"Peons can't do without me," Emmett grumbled. Nathan saw the spark in Emmett's rheumy eyes. "It's a curse, but hell. Us men got to do what needs doing. Right, men?"

Amid the quickly uttered responses of all three of them, one lone little voice piped up. "What about me?"

Emmett stopped mid-stride and stared at her. "Why, honey, you're the reason. For all of us. The *raison d'être*." He tapped gently on the crown of her head with a crooked finger. "And don't you ever forget it."

The bacon was gone and the burger attacked. They had demolished the second communal basket of fries, and there was only one big old homemade chocolate milkshake partly imbibed in front of Trasher.

She groaned and pushed it away. "Can't drink anymore."

Zach patted her hand. "Remember those words when you're sixteen, honey. Use it every half hour on evenings and weekends. Okay?"

Trasher giggled. "I'll always want chocolate shakes."

Nathan smiled. The celebration was almost over, but he was going to milk every single second. For her. He didn't mind making Og laugh either, if he could. "He's not talking about milkshakes, honey."

Zach peered at the screen of his smart phone. "Got another ding on the renter app, Nate."

Og jumped in. "Might be able to make back some of the cash we lost sending the other guy packing." He scrutinized the bill, slapped it back on the table. "Damn. The fries really were bottomless."

Nathan stared at him quizzically.

"Yeah," Zach continued. "Guy says he'll be here this week. Says he might know you."

"Well, that's good news." Nathan scooped his keys up off the table. "Any other miracles in your e-mail?"

Zach continued to scan the tiny screen. "Actually, yes. Your Aunt Tilley and your gram send their love. They e-mailed me because apparently you don't check your e-mail often enough." He chuckled. "They're definitely looking for a place now. Your gram's—"

"She told you not to say that anymore. She's your gram too. Officially. Remember?"

"Fine. Gram's apparently gotta get out of her house in a month." He looked at Nathan meaningfully.

Nathan shrugged. "Don't look at me. Gram needs a place with no stairs. We barely got through that mess in the cottage and we both agreed it's unlivable. Floors ripped up in patches, who knows what's all living in there right now. I mean, I hate this—you know me—but I'm right. It's not exactly where I'd plant two older ladies. Especially not ones I love. There are other cousins, with rooms."

Og nodded at him in approval. "Making progress."

Zach sat, one arm around the back of Trasher's chair. "Yes, on all counts. But it doesn't help me from wishing the timing was different. And not only for their sakes." He closed his eyes, rolled his head back. "Remember, Nate? Those flaky buttermilk biscuits, hot from the oven."

"Stop."

"Home-fried chicken. Not takeout and *not* franchise. But literally, dipped three times in the best stuff that," he copped a quick glance at Trasher, "ever came out of a chicken's butt, and in the residue from smashing heads of wheat. *Mmmm.*"

Trasher recoiled from his arm. "Ew. Chickens' butts? Smashing heads? What kind of weirdo *are* you?"

Og winked at her. "That would be eggs, missy, and flour."

"Oh." She got the point and glared at Zach. She poked him in the chest with her stubby finger. "Weirdo."

"She's got you pegged."

"Nathan? Nathan Gentael?"

A brawny man in brown corduroy pants and white shirt stood by their table. Nathan reached back into the distant past of his teenage years. "Jonas? Jonas Briarhedge?"

A huge smile broke out on the man's face. "It is you. How you doing, man?" His hand came around and he grabbed Nathan's with both of his, shaking hard. "It's been too long."

"I'm back. Well, we're back," he added, with a glance at Zach then a much briefer one at Og. "In the old homestead. We're fixing it up."

"Serious? Hey, that's great news. We always wanted you back, wanted the house to stay in your family. Excellent."

"You? Still out at the farm?"

"You know it. Only now, it's not a farm. Thanks to Courtney it's Briarhedge Stables. We're online, and we do some Airbnb. Horse riding, trail stuff. Even keep some tiny Asian goats."

"Sounds fantastic. And... Courtney?" His expression turned quizzical, then realization hit him. "Not Courtney from third grade? The one you couldn't stand? The one you said was the bane of your existence?"

"Apparently, I couldn't stand her so much, I had to marry her so I could keep track of where she was, and also make her promise to live with me forever until the end of time, and all that."

Forever. The end of time. The feeling stabbed through Nathan, actually weakened him.

Good thing he was sitting. He made a deliberate decision to avoid looking anywhere in Og's direction.

"Well, good for you, man," Nate proclaimed. "Sounds like you've got all your ducks in a row."

The guy's voice gentled. "Another one, now you're back." His voice dipped. "Missed you, bro. We all did. Courtney too."

"Hey, thanks. Oh, and before my manners escape me, you remember Zach from a couple summers when we were kids, right? And this here's Og, and this special young lady is—"

But having been given the stage finally, Trasher burst out something she'd apparently been holding in. "Horses?"

"Wha... oh yeah, sweetie. We've got horses. In fact, we're hoping that'll become our main business. It's doing good right now. You like horses, darlin'?"

She stared at him, then looked at Nathan, Og, then Zach, as if appealing for aid. Then she mustered up the courage as she said the sentence slowly. "I love horses."

"Well, why don't you come by and ride some time? Help with the grooming, the feeding? We can always use help. Tell you what." He leaned both hands on the table. "Come by today for a ride. Right now if you want as our welcome to Refuge Bay. If you want to do it again, one hour of farm work equals one free hour of horse riding. How's that?"

Joy lit in her face. But even as the joy appeared, Nathan's stomach constricted.

Trasher clenched her eyes shut, stayed that way for long seconds. Enough time for Nate's heart to slam in his body, fill his throat. Then she opened them again, at ease once more. Relaxed. She looked at Nathan, eyes shining. "Can I? Just for today?"

I'd make the earth split open for you, sweetness, and pour out its treasures. The heavens too, little one. Rain down on you all the gifts of a lifetime. Make dragonflies dance for you, through meadows and streams and forests. All for you.

All he said to her was, "Sure."

"Let's get our bill settled then. You can give us directions or we can follow you." Og stood, receipt in hand. "You want anything to go, honey?"

Jonah slapped an open hand onto Nathan's shoulder. "Follow us. You can meet—*re-meet*—my honey and Amelia, our baby. And you, little lady, can meet the horses you're going to be spending a lot of time with."

Chapter Sixteen

Nathan

One tired little girl slumped in the backseat of the Mustang, the rising moon casting its rays on her. What a long day it had been. Now, she was cuddled soundly into Og, his arm around her. He'd called the backseat position when he'd seen how tired she was and how much she needed sleep. He'd asked Nathan to drive his car after the crazy, long, yet wonderful day.

So full of new things for a little kid. The horse riding—she'd ridden for two straight hours, then the family barbecued and asked them to stay, and she'd giggled about the goats, petted the cows, and fed the chickens. She'd taken a dip into a fast-running stream in a borrowed bathing suit for a wash off, and called out to the men... her men... nonstop.

"Nathan. Watch me. Zach. See this. Og. Look what I can do."

It had been glorious.

Now she had one arm wrapped around Og's middle, and her whole weight was slumped onto his side over the backseat hump. Nathan glanced in the rearview mirror. Og had to be uncomfortable, but he wouldn't move to give himself relief, no matter what. Something strong compressed in Nathan's throat. Duty called, and she came first. Damn. He admired him so much. He wanted to be in Og's energy, never mind the lust Nathan locked away most of the time.

"Who knew she could ride like that?" Zach mused in the front seat beside him, sighing. "Kid's full of surprises."

Nathan nodded. "She rode her guts out today, didn't she?"

"Well, it was only on a pony, and the pony was named Gemma. Gentle, but still."

"She was eyeing that big horse, though."

Zach snorted, and his eyes widened. "Hell. That thing was a stallion."

Nathan nodded. "But she was up for it. One hundred percent. That animal scared the willies out of me."

"It kinda gave you an *I'll kick you* look, didn't it?"

Nathan laughed, shook his head. "I'll have to see it again sometime when we're there and she wants to…" He caught himself, pushed down the sharp pang. "Well, later. When we're visiting sometime."

An uncomfortable silence, soaked with meaning, fell in the car. Zach broke it when he whispered, "I wish—"

Nathan cut him off. "I know what you wish. I wish it too. It's not to be, though."

They exited onto the country road, and then turned into the little roundabout in the back of the house.

"We're home," Nathan called softly, hoping to jog Trasher out of the vise grip she had on Og. The man needed a break. Nathan gazed around the yard, already finding it more homey than it had been for days. For the first time really.

Of course, Zach was always around, but with Trasher and Og here, it was the thing he would never have: family.

Something jolted him as he looked around. Something was different.

The mess they'd left in the yard, in the middle of it actually, was cleaned up, the tools stacked off by Manor House.

They hadn't left it like that.

Over to the right, to the little cottage that definitely wasn't in shape to house anybody, let alone the likes of his old aunt and Gram, had shining windows. The front porch roof was straight, and that damn thing had been lopsided and ready to cave in when they'd checked it out. The post was new, and a bit rough-hewn, but it was in place, strong and sturdy.

There was a pile of boards stacked beside the porch, ready to patch the hole. There were tiny furrows in the dirt to the right, looking like a makeshift blueprint.

At the main house, the tiny stone back stoop was swept. The bits of sage that the child had plucked from under the window yesterday, which had dried when she left them in her upset, were gone. There was a huge pile of junk, a good distance from the cottage, of old furniture and other crap. Ratty, torn, and dusty, they hadn't been able to sit on the stuff, it had been such a mess. Worse, it had stunk. Badly. Musty and raw.

Like shit, Gram would have cheerfully announced, rolling it off her tongue for extra emphasis. She might've repeated it a few times. She did like her swearwords, and shocking people.

"Hey. What gives?" Zach had caught on, and whispered his surprise.

"We'd better be careful." Nathan laid a finger on his lips. *Shhh.*

"Yeah." Zach snorted. "Because whoever tidied up everything and stacked the garbage neatly—they might be dangerous. Seriously? Somebody does all that to our place he's not going to conk us on the head and make off with our treasures. We don't have any, remember?" He sighed. "Let's go."

"But—"

"No buts. Come on." They got out of the car.

"Guys. I'll let her sleep for a few more," Og said from the backseat. He hadn't noticed anything yet from his vantage point, slouched as he was to make it more comfortable for Trasher.

Zach bent to his window. "Okay. We'll be back in a couple of minutes. We'll carry her in, if need be. You won't have to read her any stock market stories tonight." He smiled.

"Did you tell him?"

Tell him what, Nathan thought. He didn't think he could take any more bad news.

Zach shook his head. "We managed fine. I think you and I can handle this."

They entered the house cautiously. They hadn't locked it—*stupid*—and now they might be paying for it.

"Look," Zach whispered and pointed at the kitchen counter. "There."

One quiche, perfectly baked, sat on the counter under a couple of layers of cheesecloth.

Nathan whispered back. "Does that mean the burglar has good taste and left your quiche uneaten?"

Zach smacked him. "No, you dork. There were two."

"The plot thickens."

"You check out the front room and I'll go upstairs."

A momentary pang hit him as he thought of his studio.

He couldn't bear for anybody to find it, see his stuff, or worse—tamper with it. All the feelings from his wonderful past engulfed him. It would kill him if somebody stumbled upon his art. It would be like sharing a piece of his soul.

Tomorrow he'd burn every damn thing in the studio.

A thorough search of the rest of the house turned up with nothing, which made him uneasy. Someone had been there, but there was no evidence except a missing quiche.

He met Zach in the kitchen. "We've left Og out there long enough with the kid." Nathan moved to the kitchen window, craned his neck, and peered outside. "Looks like they're both asleep."

"Well, I'm not carrying him in." Zach gave Nathan a look then asked, "You checked the basement?"

Nathan shook his head.

"The barn?"

"Nope."

The cottage?"

Nathan slumped. "No. Let's go."

They started with the tiny cottage, where they got their answer. On an old sleeping bag, stretched out, was the renter they'd turned away earlier. He was snoring, the empty pie plate and a fork beside him.

"Bugger him. He got into our wine." One of their precious few bottles of wine sat beside him—a gift from Tilson Wineries—with a plastic Cinderella cup beside it. Zach looked ready to charge him.

Nathan put a restraining hand on Zach's forearm. Only about a glass and a half was missing from the bottle. "After all the work he's done, he can bloody well have the whole bottle, don't you think?"

Zach remained upset. He walked over to the sleeping man and, to Nathan's surprise, kicked the guy's boot.

"Wha—Oh, say. Hey." The man pulled himself up and rested on two elbows. He had the most gloriously blue eyes Nathan had ever seen.

"Who the hell are you and what are you doing sleeping in our house?"

"Too late for nursery tales, man. No bears around here. Ditto on Goldi." The guy ignored Zach's question, and instead rubbed his beard slowly. He took a slurp out of the Cinderella cup, poured a bit more into it, sloshed it around, and downed it before looking up at the two of them. "Oh hell, my manners. Sorry. Want some?"

"No, we're—"

"No, we bloody well don't," Zach snapped. "Who are you, and what are you doing here?"

A deep sigh. "I don't want trouble. I just…." He looked up at Zach and Nate beseechingly. "I really need a place, guys. I thought if I cleaned up and did what I could, you'd see I was reliable. Decent. That I'd started contributing already." A sheepish look crossed his face. "No money, fellas. Not a dime." He took a long look at Zach's face, stared into his eyes, and the blue darkened. Clouded over.

Then he rousted himself. "But I see that's not the case. Okay. I'll be on my way. The sleeping bag is yours. Found it in the barn. I can't pay for the quiche—damn incredible, by the way—but I'll get off your property immediately."

"You don't need to—" Nathan started, but Zach cut him off.

Zach did an about-face. "Don't go." He grabbed the man's arm, halting him. "The least we can do for you, after all your work…. Oh hell. Stay the night."

"You sure? You can check my references online. I'm safe. Disgustingly so."

"Let's sit down. Come outside."

The three men sat. The stranger, on the porch. Nathan on the woodpile, and Zach drew himself up, cross-legged, on a flat stone in front of the cottage.

Nathan peeked at the car. Empty. Og must have carried Trasher in and put her to bed. Had he noticed all the changes in the deepening dark?

They both stared at the handsome stranger and waited.

"Name's Galen Tilth. Actually, Galen Odin Watshammer Tilth. Yeah, don't laugh. My parents were into Norse mythology and I got stuck with the name. Don't even get me started on the short form for Odin. Thank god, they made it one of my middle names. I never tell anyone." He looked around, not particularly at anything, but seemingly at everything. "My story's no biggie. I didn't kill a man, I'm not running. I didn't do time. I want peace and quiet, and I'm willing to contribute." He sighed. "No, scratch that. Need to. As you no doubt can see."

"What the hell were you in the past, the EverReady bunny?" Zach snorted.

"I did construction work on the side, and it became a passion. Dad's in construction. I worked for his company."

"Can we see ID? Where do we find you online?"

"Tilth Construction."

The answer came easy enough, but Nathan detected the stranger was holding back. Hiding something.

Galen shifted, reached into his back pocket, and pulled out a well-used leather wallet. "Take a look. All there."

Nathan looked through it and found the usual ID, but no photos and no indication there was someone to contact in case of an emergency. For a person who could ingratiate himself so quickly and had such an easy way about him, something was definitely off.

Nathan didn't want any surprises. He'd carefully made the last few years of his life surprise free. He glanced over at Zach. He'd been tired earlier, but now he was curiously alert. Every muscle in his body taut, and he had an odd energy about him. Huh. Maybe Galen was ticking Zach's boxes.

"Looks in order," Nathan said, handing the wallet back to Galen. "We'll get you some blankets from the house, a pillow. Maybe we can work something out. Perhaps you can stay in the cottage for now if you're willing to contribute, providing you check out."

He gave a quick glance over to Zach, sensing his assent, then continued.

"We'll let you know for sure in the morning. Oh, and there's another man on site too. Og Reiden. There's also a little girl, though she's here only until tomorrow. One thing you need to know, up front, with her here, we toe the line. One hundred percent family friendly, nothing untoward. No cursing or veiled references. Even if you think you're alone, she has the craziest habit of popping up where you don't expect her. We don't want trouble, but if we see any, we won't hesitate to toss you out." He paused for effect. "Got it?" He searched the man's face. "Understand?"

"Hell yeah." His expression hardened. "Kids are sacred. Anyone does anything to your kid, any kid, I'm right there with you."

"Good. I think we're done for now. We'll bring the stuff out for you. Thanks for what you did around here. It's actually quite unbelievable."

Galen flushed, the red moving up around the bristles of his five o'clock shadow. "Well, that's good," he sputtered, then collected himself. "One thing, though."

"Yeah?"

"Is the person who made that quiche on site? I'd like to do some bowing. Whoever made that is inspired."

Zach snorted. "Done PR on the side, have you?"

"You?"

"Yeah. I threw some stuff together. No big deal. This and that from the garden, some farm eggs. Bit of ham, home cured, from another neighbor. Chopped up celery, onion from the market, and as they say—special spices."

"Great pastry."

"Someone's gram taught me and warned if I didn't make it exactly her way and do it right, she'd come back and haunt me."

"Pastry boot camp." Galen grinned, a sparkle in his beautiful eyes. Nathan admired the raw good looks of the man. Not that he was interested—which surprised him—and worried him.

A quick glance at his Zach, who'd caught Galen's zing.

Galen got up, brushed off his ass, and Nathan watched Zach follow Galen's movements.

"Well, if anyone else tastes that, you'll have a run on all your rooms, finished or not," Galen said. "People will be lining up outside. A pie kitchen." He smiled at them once more, but one with tinges of something buried.

If he checked out, his secrets were his to keep. They had another set of hands, and this guy knew what he was doing.

Galen directed his last comments to Zach. "I suggest you send any leftover quiche, once your little girl and the rest of you are done with it, out my way. Hate waste." He grinned, and Zach seemed a little dumbstruck before he got up and walked toward the house.

Chapter Seventeen

Og

Og carried the tired little girl with the peaceful smile up the stairs. It was no secret she'd been getting under his skin in the worst way possible. The heartfelt way. The way she lay limp in his arms, completely trusting, something deep in him stirred, and he imagined this was what it felt like to have a daughter.

He tried to push the thoughts and feelings away. She had to be put to bed, tucked in. He was only doing what was essential and decent. He was always good at doing what had to be done, and he could always be counted on.

But the feeling wouldn't leave.

Every action he took made the feelings more indelible. From holding her super close while he bent to pull back the covers with one hand, then laying her gently on the antique bed, seeing her body relax comfortably as she landed on the mattress. Pulling off her shoes, her socks.

Running to the bathroom, he filled her glass—another Darth Vader special—with water, making sure it was ice cold, then he went back into her bedroom and placed it on the nightstand. He calculated how far away it needed to be so if she accidentally turned over and thrashed or hugged her pillow weird, it wouldn't spill.

Then he watched her for a few moments, breathing deep, utterly lost in dreamland. "Good night, princess," he whispered. Tiptoeing out, he quietly pulled her door shut, then at the last minute left it open the tiniest crack, so if she cried out, they'd hear and could come running.

He stood outside her door. His heart beating a bit hard. Everything necessary, everything she'd required had been done.

Realization flooded through him.

That was his little girl in there. *His* freakin' little girl.

And his partner—*his partner, dear god almighty*—was downstairs taking care of business with his best friend. Nathan had encouraged Trasher all day. Had spent the first half hour of her horse ride beside her, his hands up on the saddle and lightly on her back because she didn't want him to let her go when they'd put her on Gemma. She was scared to be up there. Og had seen the strain on Nathan's face, the pain from maintaining that awkward position, but he persisted.

She'd wanted to ride, so badly, and after all the bluster about how much she loved horses and how good she was at it, she couldn't bear to lose face, and she'd appealed to Nathan—her other *dad*— with a desperate look.

The man had such a heart. He could see beneath the surface, and respond the way people needed. Sensitive, but not weak, Nathan stood up for the principles he believed in, and had no trouble putting Og in his place. Not many people tried, and those who did stopped and stuttered. Not Nathan, who didn't give ground, made his case, and wouldn't back down.

A thought Og never would've believed he'd entertain took up residence in his brain. Maybe he should settle down here, with Nathan.

Og wrapped his palm around the banister at the head of the stairs and stopped. The thought didn't seem so crazy. He was tired of the one-night stands and hadn't indulged in many for a long time.

This outpost from the world felt good, and right, and, yeah, a bit weird, but comforting at the same time.

His cell vibrated. The Watcher.

He strode quickly to the end of the hallway, stared out the window. Nathan, Zach, and another guy were out by the cottage talking. Perfect. Engaged and out of the house.

Og slid his finger to accept the call. "Reiden."

"Subject located. Orange level. Proceed?"

Orange level. *Shit*. Next to Red. Only one level worse than that. Black.

"Proceed. Quit the commando talk and tell me how and where my brother is."

The sharp cadence of the Watcher's voice always got to him. The man had a reputation for being deadly straight, honest, and the best in locating people who vaporized. "Your brother's been located deep in a jungle that's not even on the map in South American near the equator. The locals call it Dust Valley."

Huh? Jungles were lush and green. "Why Dust Valley?"

"Because everything that goes in stays for eternity, as dust."

Okay. Not good. "Who's got him?"

"When your brother couldn't get into the military, he joined a fringe militia group. Turns out they're not fringe, they're drug runners. For whatever their reasons, they thought he was a plant. He couldn't convince them otherwise, and gotta say, there's no easy way to tell you this: he's being tortured."

Og's gut roiled and he felt the bile work its way up his throat, but he got the necessary words out, choked as they were. "What's the next step?"

"I have an in with a couple of locals. Intelligence indicates that the drug runners are not in one place for longer than a couple of days. I need to ascertain their next planned move, and as soon as I have a plan of action I'll let you know." He had the grace to pause. "It won't be cheap."

"It doesn't matter. Do it."

"Expect more information in four to seven days. I'll be in touch as soon as I know. Don't contact me unless it's critical, and then make sure you do. Next payment will be due then. I'll send details the regular way."

"Understood."

The Watcher hung up while Og's torture went into high gear.

***

Nathan

Nathan and Zach walked into the main house after they concluded their discussion with Galen. Zach headed straight for his room and shut the door, and Nathan glanced at Og, his expression serious as he paced the kitchen.

"Is she...." Nathan stopped, stared at him. "What's wrong?"

"She's in bed. Sound asleep."

"Then why are you upset?"

Og's eyes narrowed, flicked off to the side. "That antique you got over there is flashing."

Nathan's brows lifted. "The agency called the answering machine?" Hell. They were due here in the morning. Why on earth would they be bothering them now? Was there some kind of trouble, or worse, had they found out something more about her background that changed how the matter was going to be handled?

Fear sliced through him. If only he could keep her.

Og laid a restraining hand on his forearm and Nathan sighed, a space hollowed out where his stomach used to be. Og sat at the table beside him, stretching his fingers out, then relaxing them over and over again.

Zach came out of his room, stopped, and stared at them. "What's happening?"

"Phone call. The agency. Something's off."

With his back rigid, Zach planted himself beside Og. They waited, wordless, their expressions grim.

Nathan went to the machine and hit play. He couldn't believe what they were hearing.

"Hello, Mr. Gentael, this is Hanna Pottsfield from Child Protective Services. The foster home we had arranged is out of the question due to a family illness. At the present time, we don't have any empty beds in our group homes. We talked to the references you submitted on behalf of yourself, Mr. Reiden, and Mr. Lees. We ran background checks on each of you, and since they're in good order we wondered if you'd be willing to keep the child for at least the next couple of weeks. We'll be by each week to check on you, and we'll call regularly to keep you updated on any potential foster homes. Please call me back as soon as you get this message to discuss attending classes to become a foster care-giver." Beep.

"What?" Og sputtered.

"Holy hell." Zach jumped up and practically danced in place. "Of course. For however long they want. For-fucking-ever."

A reprieve. They'd been given a reprieve. "I'll call them in the morning."

"Hell no," Og ordered. "Call them now and leave a message, then call in the morning, too. Don't stop calling until you speak to that woman, and have her send you an email capturing everything she told you. You need that shit in writing, man."

Nathan picked up his phone, his fingers shaking.

Everything was falling into place. He couldn't believe it, but everything was falling into place.

He kept thinking the same thing, half an hour later, up in his bedroom when he shrugged off his shirt and tossed it beside the bed. If Galen worked out, they had a renter. Well, the guy couldn't pay them, but he could work hard and he was brilliant with construction. They would save money. He was a godsend.

Christ, he hoped Galen being there didn't squirrel the deal with CPS. It shouldn't. Galen lived in the cottage, separate and far enough away from the house to be another property if they didn't have so much land.

What about Og? Nathan let his imagination get the best of him. He looked at the bed and pictured Og there, enticing and inviting. Not for one night, but for…the foreseeable future. Nathan didn't have any illusions they'd be together forever, but maybe they could have a good run. A year or two.

He blinked. What the hell was he thinking? He knew that wasn't for him anymore. He'd sworn off relationships.

He crawled into bed alone, pulled up the covers, and slapped the pillow around under his head, until he got it the way he wanted it.

Bright side: Trasher was staying. For another few weeks, and Og and Zach wanted that. They'd take care of her and protect her. Help her get her feet under her, and maybe she'd tell them her real name and where she was from.

In this moment, everything was perfect. The Refuge Bay community had welcomed him back and shown their support when he bought the house. They wanted him to renovate it and bring it back to life.

Even on the home front, things were looking up with his parents. He'd gotten a message from Mom earlier, and she was doing well. Dad was taking it easy—doctor's orders—and was working part time.

Best of all, Nathan had finally carved out a dream he'd started to manifest, make it real. Buying this house, this property, keeping it afloat had been difficult, and he'd scraped and saved and killed himself to do it. The new him, the non-artist, had made it happen.

Sure, he missed painting, but he'd had to make a choice—wallow or make his life mean something.

Manor House was going to actually be what he'd dreamt of: a place for broken souls to come and recover. A place where he could do some good, and be the man he wanted to become. The one who, when he died, people would remember and love.

"Don't forget to check out the potential renter," Zach called through the door. "Message the guy. Grab him while he's hot. Then we'll have two. Okay?"

"Will do, buddy. 'Night."

Nate picked up his iPad, worked his way through to the rental app. Found the line that proclaimed *YOU HAVE A RENTER*, and clicked on the link.

Terror crept up from the base of his spine, radiated, jagged and ugly, through him. It grabbed him in its bony, relentless fingers and squeezed.

A familiar picture stared out at him, harsh.

Elliot Overbrand.

The man he'd spent years running from.

The man who'd been in his nightmares too long. That emotionless face, those relentless eyes. The bastard who'd destroyed his and his parents' lives and hadn't stopped until they were devastated and crushed.

Somehow, that piece of shit had found him again.

Now, the last little bits of life Nathan had been able to scrounge together were in jeopardy.

Worse, so were the lives of all the people he loved most in the world.

Zach. Og. Little Trasher were all fair game.

Chapter Eighteen

Nathan

Nathan moaned, tossed and turned. There was nothing left for him to do except to let the nightmare play out. It started as it always did with something beautiful. So beautiful it was practically a gift from the gods.

He'd known his talent, his gift, had come from an elevated place, a noble place, and he honored the gift. The painting had come together in his mind's eye and it flowed effortlessly onto the canvas. He saw it on a wall in a museum. On a postcard. A flash of it on TV, in a commercial. It started to appear everywhere, but he couldn't quite capture the focal point of it when he woke. That was still eluding him.

The dream shifted, becoming a playback of what happened five years ago when he'd taken the leap and started working on his dream. Eager to cull from the ether the painting that haunted him, called to him.

When he'd finally started it, the creation of it had consumed him, but as he worked on it, more of it came into view. It was stunning. A man's heart serving as a hazy backdrop, faint, but alive. The man's body, ordinary, his muscles and energy focused toward the bottom right-hand corner. In that corner was the love that would make his life worthwhile.

He'd been working furiously in his studio, snatching sleep when he had to, working at times thirty-six hours straight. Inspiration flowed through him and he'd sketched and planned. He'd even started all number of other paintings too, in the lulls. Some erotic, some not. *The show he would create and have, the exhibition that would bring his work to the world, had started to become reality.*

In that fury of activity, the answer to that one painting started to reveal itself. The first piece had shown itself to him so long ago. Now the culmination of it was going to be revealed. He knew it. He felt it. The revelation was almost his.

Then he'd heard the sob and rushed into the family room as his mom came rushing out of it. He grabbed her, held her. She gave him a watery smile and wiped the tears from her face, assuring him there was no trouble, but he saw the wild look behind the smile and wouldn't let her go.

They were behind on the mortgage. They were close to losing their home, his childhood home, their lifetime refuge. When he pressed her for the reason why, in her determination to not tell him, he knew why. He was the cause of their ruin.

He'd come out about a year earlier, and the hate aimed at him and his family had started with his art. A few hateful, small-minded townspeople slowly, with determination, instigated a boycott of the town's favorite doctor. The man who'd birthed their children, tended their skinned knees, and healed them when they were ill was shunned because of his son.

Nathan had run to his studio, taken one last look at the piece that had literally been burning in him all his life, and picked up a knife and slashed at the painting of the man that had been calling to him since he was a teen. He started at that heart, the focal point of the painting, and curiously, the knife wouldn't pierce the canvas. Angry, all the more determined, he'd pushed harder, and it finally split.

He started again, focusing at the bottom right corner, putting muscle into it. The canvas tore until the wall showed through.

He wanted to destroy it, but realized if he did it would be nothing more than another destroyed canvas, and the lesson would fade.

No, he decided, sitting there on the floor of his studio, the sweat pouring off him, the anger, the self-recrimination replacing the blood in his veins, he wanted enough of the original painting to stay intact so he could always know what he had destroyed: his parents' lives and their whole world.

When he'd left the studio that day, his reason for art died. He could never be who he really was. His loving parents moved to a tiny apartment claiming that they loved it. They didn't need the aggravation of maintaining a big house. They refused to take any more he offered, and encouraged him to enrich himself, and live. Live big, son, they'd said.

He would spend the rest of his life paying back that love. Since they wouldn't take anything from him, he'd help other broken men. Give them the home base, the support to find love, to live their passions as he'd had.

Nathan had penance to pay. Every day. The hugeness of it, though, threatened to crush him every time he started to think of it, so he didn't.

In case he ever forgot, though, he regularly viewed the canvases, ran his fingers along them, especially along the top of that one. See again the knife lying in front of it, the dust gathering on it like a relic in a display case. To see the paintbrushes standing in the glass jar beside it, the paint dried hard on their tips, the water long evaporated. To remember.

A sound, perhaps the wind, woke him and it took a moment for him to remember he was in his bedroom, back in Manor House. He'd bought it, had plans, and he was fine. He started to swallow, and found his throat dry with grit.

"Enough. Gotta get out of here," he muttered to himself and glanced at his watch. Four a.m. He needed to spin off this negative energy, then come back and try to catch a couple of hours of real sleep.

He got up, determined to find an answer to the returning threat.

Elliot Overbrand wouldn't hesitate to involve Trasher. He would hurt her. There was no limit to his cruelty.

Nathan ran down the stairs and slammed into a hard wall of man.

Og stood in front of him, his expression angry and grim.

"You've got some explaining to do."

"What?"

"You've been holding out on me. We gotta talk."

"What do you mean?"

"You're freaking out about something. Don't try to hide it from me. What's wrong?"

Nathan glared at Og. "Pot. Kettle. You don't look too good yourself. What the hell is wrong with you?"

Og shook his head impatiently. "I'm fine. What bothers me is when someone I'm in a business relationship with holds back important information." The pallor of his face didn't match his tough words.

And... *business* relationship?

"That's all this is to you? A business relationship?" Nathan bit out. "Then what the hell was that kiss earlier, and the one a couple days ago, right here in this hallway, right up there? What the fuck was that?"

He thought the vein in Og's forehead would burst. "You, you..."

Then he felt his world spin right off its axis as Og grabbed him harshly and crushed him to his chest, his savage words rushing into Nate's brain. "I need you. Now. No more fucking around. Now." Blistering heat coursed through him, almost making him lose his balance.

Finally. They were admitting it. Holy shit, they were admitting it.

"That can be arranged," Nathan rasped out. "I'm ready." His hand reached down, found the bulge of Og's thick, hard cock, and his fingers curved around it.

A sharp intake and a jagged quiver from Og's frame showed how badly he was trying to fight his response. He moaned. "Then take this." Og pushed against him.

In the haze of his arousal, Nathan suddenly remembered something important—the only thing that could have forced him to stop. He pulled away from Og, keeping him at arm's length. "What the hell are we thinking?"

"We're thinking... Oh fuck." Nathan could see the exact moment Og caught on. The color drained from his face and he stuttered two steps back. "Shit. No."

Nathan was still breathing hard. "Yeah. She's asleep, but she could get up any moment. Fuck. This is so not happening. Not here."

Og stared, as if trying to see Nate's thoughts. Determination sparked in his face. He grabbed Nathan's shoulders, physically turned him around, then leaned in close, whispering roughly, "Get up there. To your room."

"Then you bloody well better be following me."

The warning landed right in Nathan's ear, hot and teasing. Promising dark delights. "Oh, if you don't get a move on, I'll be there before you, and if that happens, you're getting a spanking."

Nathan didn't have to be told twice. Or hell, even once for that matter. He tore up the stairs. In less than a minute he was in his room, on the mattress, flat on his back.

Og clicked the door lock shut, then moved to the bed, wicked authority in his stance. He looked down with a smile. Then Og dropped his thin pajamas, and they pooled at his feet.

Nathan got his first glimpse of him bare. Og's cock had a slight curve and was aimed right at him. The slit was moist, precum glistening at its tip. The long, thick length of him left Nathan breathless and he swallowed.

Apparently, Og wasn't going to give it up so easy. His eyebrow arched, and he gave Nathan a supremely confident, cocky look. Like he knew he held the prize, bobbing in front of Nathan's mouth. Og's scent, spice with heavy musk, filled Nathan's senses. He'd be surprised if the whole house wasn't rife with it.

Og's gaze narrowed. The smile disappeared. "Are you ready?"

Nathan nodded, the simple act of speaking suddenly beyond him.

Og took a step forward, bringing his thighs to the edge of the bed. "Saving your mouth for better things?"

Their gazes locked, and Nathan nodded again…slowly.

"Well, good then." Og's hands tightened on his hips, fingers splayed. "Are you ready to blow me?"

Hell. Nathan thought he'd weaken from the order, which intensified the fierce lust raging through him. Og's hard cock in his mouth, sliding up and down his waiting throat, was everything he wanted. "Yes."

"Of course you are." Og's expression was smug, but there was something behind it as well. Pain? Nathan felt a flash of confusion, but he was in it now. Og continued with the next directive. "There's going to be no messing around tonight." His knee hit the bed, then somehow he was over Nathan's chest, straddling him. The tip of that bobbing cock at his lips.

Nathan was pinned to the bed. He craned his neck forward, mouth open, lips waiting.

But Og's cock was out of reach. "Please," he whispered.

Og exhaled a short burst of air. "It's right there. Come for it. It's all yours, if you can reach it."

Nathan strained forward, but the bastard didn't help out, not an inch. He kept straddling him with his beefy hands on his hips, his moss green eyes practically glowing.

"I-I can't. You're too heavy. I can't reach."

"You want me to come closer?" Og shifted forward, and if anything, felt heavier now. Nathan was even more pinned to the bed. The smell of him was intoxicating, overpowering.

Nate shut his eyes, imagined the tantalizing tip on his lips. He knew it would be firm but with the power of steel behind it. "Come closer."

Og moved closer, but still kept his dick out of reach. "What do you want me to do to you? Tell me." The authority in his voice was undeniable.

Shivers ran through Nathan. His own cock was weeping. He could barely hold back from blowing his load. But he'd take care of Og first, do him, then Og would take care of him.

"I'm waiting. If I don't hear from you soon, I'm strapping on those pants and you'll never get this bad boy. Ever."

Nate knew it was a game, but somehow it didn't feel like one anymore. "No. I...I want you to fuck my mouth. Please. *Please*."

Og groaned, his expression held tension in every line, every feature. "That's more like it. Here." He loosened his ab muscles and jutted forward. "Have a lick."

Finally, that beautiful cock was in front of his lips. Nathan craned his neck forward and stuck out his tongue. *Yes. Ambrosia.* A tiny mewling erupted from his throat, but he didn't care.

"Closer. I don't want to just lick you all night, damn it. Stop playing with me, for fuck's sake. Open my lips with it."

"With?"

"Your cock."

A masterful smile. Then Og moved higher on his chest, held that swaying cock in front of him, angled it downward, and pressed it against Nate's lips. That gorgeous cock parted his lips, pushed them aside, and entered. He felt the full force of the man and his power.

He was overwhelmed by how much Og made him feel. Having Og's fantastic cock in his mouth, surrendering to the deep thrusts and closeness of it all...it was almost too much.

Overwhelmed, Nate did something he knew he should never do. Especially not at this moment. "I love you."

Nathan froze once those words spilled out of his mouth, and was surprised when, seconds later, he felt tender fingers brush hair from his forehead. Then, said so softly that he had to strain to hear, Og whispered, "I care about you, too." The words were guttural, but that made it all the more touching.

Not love, but for real, the man wanted him. Nate could feel it. Og was hot and heavy with it, mindless.

"Now," Nathan said, an earnest plea. "Fuck me, babe. Fuck me hard."

Og jammed his cock down Nate's throat, but he could tell the man held back. They hadn't had that conversation yet. Despite Nathan egging him on, begging him, Og was still restrained.

Because he cared for him. He'd just told him that.

Nate knew how he felt. He'd deny it in the morning. None of this was in his life plan. Especially now when he was once again a marked man. But right now, in this moment, he knew the truth, and he'd enjoy it.

***

Og

I care about you, too.

What the hell was *that*? Years ago, Og had decided he wasn't going to let his feelings enter into this relationship or into any relationship ever again. He was a free agent, a free spirit, and would always stay that way. Even if he had been thinking of making this place with Nathan his final destination, the one where he'd live and settle and grow old...all that was off the table now because of Michael.

He had to find his brother, and nothing, no other attachment, could interfere with that.

Not the sweet little girl he'd tucked into bed who already trusted him more than he deserved. Not the poet who'd surprised him with his mettle and soothed him with his kind soul.

Not wacky Zach, either. The man who loved Nathan as much as Og did, but not in *that* way, thank god.

None of it. None of it was for him.

So what was he doing here, now?

God, he cared about this man. Why was he leading him on?

Nathan sucked in and drew Og's dick farther into his mouth. He strained to get his arms around him, but Og slapped them down. He wouldn't permit that. This way was better.

He couldn't stop himself from falling into the act until the only thing that existed were him and the man currently sending him to heights he couldn't remember ever reaching before.

The sucking, the pulling. The slick wetness. This guy could give blowjobs for a living, and he'd be famous for them. Men from all over the world would come for them, would line up outside, brave the whipping winds and the freezing weather all for those lips. That incredible tension, the world-spinning manipulation.

The tension grew unbearable. In this moment, Og was consumed. The urge raced to a critical level, and if he'd wanted out, that option was long gone. He lunged forward, shoved his cock in deeper, the anguish rappelling him forward.

As if in a dream he thought he'd never have satisfied, Nathan also moved forward. To him. He let out the most ferocious fucking whisper he'd ever ejected. Thank god he remembered the kid as delirium hit him, and the rightness of bathing Nathan's mouth with his cum. He spilled himself down that throat that was opening larger for him, to receive him, fully, and he emptied himself into him.

All of him.

Og barely had time to be satiated. He'd blown his load, his muscles were spent, and his body was limp. If he could hover here for a moment or a decade….

Nathan hadn't come. He'd made Og jerk, lurch, and scandalously explode, and had taken it so perfectly—even made him feel like he wanted more. All he could give, endlessly.

Og had to take care of him. He rolled and slapped a sweaty arm over Nathan's chest, felt the soft scratch of his chest hair. "We gotta do you."

Incredibly, Nathan shook his head. "Come down first."

"But—"

"I can handle it. Don't worry, I'm still hard for you. But…."

No no no. He raked his hand down over Nathan's six pack, felt the indent where his muscles were, the glorious hardness. Then down, closer to the dark growth out of which protruded that beautiful cock.

"Gonna slip that baby into fifth gear." His fingers curved around it, and Nathan groaned, tensing all over. He copped a glance at his face, saw the wince. The intensity had to feel almost too much, and Og felt the joy deep in his chest. "Getting to you, am I?"

"One look at you and I'm hard."

An odd feeling of joy made his chest expand. "You mean that, don't you?" Og whispered.

"Of course. Hell knows I didn't want this, but where you're concerned…."

"Then let's ride, baby. All the way." Og clenched his eyes shut, but sparks danced behind his lids. "Ride for me."

Og pulled the pre-cum down Nathan's tip, slicked his cock with it. Nathan groaned and shifted, moving into place, pressing his dick up and forward to get tighter into Og's grip. He obliged and closed his eyes, felt the slippery slide of it, with just enough tension to know he was really hanging on to Nathan's cock.

Shit. He finally had his hand on poet-boy's cock.

Nathan was gripping the bedsheets, his eyes clenched tight, his jaw set, as he moved with Og's rhythms. "Just like that. Oh god. Oh god."

"Feel good, baby?" Og tightened his grip, eased his thumb at exactly the spot underneath where he knew it would blow Nathan's mind.

"Oh. My. God."

"This too." He cupped his balls, created the tension he knew Nathan would love. "Like this?"

"Oh my—"

The next thing he knew, Nathan reached up, yanked him down, and Nathan's lips were on Og's. Urgent, thrusting. Exploring his mouth voraciously, while Og felt his body tighten up, the tension ramp up to almost unbearable. "Shit. I'm gonna come again."

Nathan reach down and cupped him greedily in mid-writhe. "You do that."

In answer, Og plunged his tongue deep into Nathan's mouth. Nathan moaned and worked his balls furiously, made them burn. The heat…Og couldn't take it anymore.

A mind-blowing thought rushed through his blur of pleasure. *Together. We're gonna come together.* Need pitched in his belly, raced to lust. And then the universe stopped as this hot man gave it up for him. Came, all over his hand. Volumes, it seemed. Spilling himself endlessly.

Og couldn't hold back any longer. With a strangled cry, he arched into Nathan's grip, cursed the man who'd taken him over without his say-so, and released the last bits of his soul into Nathan's talented hand.

***

Nathan

They lay beside each other, audibly breathing hard.

"Holy fuck." Og was barely able to get words out.

"That good?"

"I don't even have the fucking energy to look at you. What the hell do you think?"

A tiny smirk hit Nate's lips. "That I surprised you?"

"There's an understatement. You're getting a chastity belt. One key. And you know who's going to be holding it."

Nathan snorted, laughed. The play, the fun. Oh, for sure, the hot sex and the lust—but the play. That was what this was all about. He'd barely remembered what it was like, it had been so long, but now it all came back.

"Thank god we came to our senses before something stupid happened on the stairs." Og drew his shoulders up to his neck then released them with a loud exhale. "Can't have the kid knowing. Advertising liaisons is never a good idea."

There was the stab. The one Nathan realized he'd been steeling himself for. With it, the thoughts he no longer wanted started their mindless whisper.

Overbrand is back.

Move on. Now. Move on.

Sell.

Pick up and run.

God, there's nowhere to run. If that bastard finds me here....

Og. He doesn't really want me....

The last one jarred him. Worse than the rest. A hit in his solar plexus, and one Nate didn't know if he could recover from. It brought him back to this moment with the man he'd admitted having fallen in love with.

How many times had he been in this spot before? Not knowing if the man he'd shared his body with, and whose body he'd explored in return, had had the same experience as him.

Sharing his body wasn't merely a release. Sure, there was that, and it had been damn good, but as he'd grown older, the other questions had started to mean more to him. In fact, they started to mean everything to him. *Do we love each other? Do we like each other? Do we have a future?*

Usually, the answer was immediate and definite.

Hey, man, great sex. Awesome blowjob. Where'd you learn to do that? A laugh. Then the guy would get dressed, perhaps find his underwear with another laugh, tug them on, shimmy into his pants, and then find his shirt, and pull it on, tuck it in. His gaze would go blank.

But Nate saw underneath the carefully calculated, overtly unhurried movements, the urgency to be somewhere else. Anywhere else. Often, out trolling again.

He'd known what it had all meant.

Absolutely nothing.

And he didn't want that anymore.

Nate glanced to his left at Og in all his naked splendor beside him. All muscle, the sheen of sweat still coating him. A naked boxer, his muscles honed to perfection. Nathan closed his eyes, finding himself waiting for the inevitable *see you later*, in some form or another.

Soon, Og would be searching for his pants.

Nate felt movement on the bed, down around his hips. Og's hand shimmied over the sheets, met his. Then Og played with his fingers, grasped his hand. Squeezed, holding on tight. Nathan couldn't breathe.

Og rattled Nathan's hand a bit. "So, what has you in a knot?"

"Huh?"

"Nothing's changed from before, you know. You were still upset earlier, and you're still gonna tell me why."

"I...." Nathan hesitated for too long.

"Damn you." Og sat up, though he was still gripping his hand, his gaze laser-focused. "I know about Overbrand. Zach checked to see who the guy was, the one who asked about the room. He did a double take. I thought he was gonna lose his quiche. I asked him what the hell was going on and he rifled around in a box in the corner, then handed me a file." Og's expression turned stern, but Nathan thought he saw more than that too. Pain. "Why the hell didn't you tell me about all this?"

Of course, he should've. The investment wasn't solid. Og was at risk. But Nate hadn't thought… "I'm sorry. We'll work something out so you get your money back, no matter what. I didn't know. I thought I'd disappeared so completely that he'd never find me. You have to believe me."

A completely dumbfounded look crossed Og's features. "The hell? The absolute, bloody hell? You think this is about business?"

"Well, we do have a business relationship, first and foremost. Your investment. So…"

And then, the man he loved—the man he didn't want to love but did—released his hand. Og let him go as if Og had been burnt, scalded from the touch.

He got off the bed, pulled his PJ pants on without a word, grabbed his t-shirt, yanked it on, and stalked out of the room without looking back.

Chapter Nineteen

Og

Well, that was a deep, steaming pile of shit. Og tore down the stairs, through the kitchen, and out the back door. He didn't slam anything, though he really wanted to, because the kid needed her sleep after all the horse-riding stuff, and that still mattered, even if all hell was raining down around him.

The cool night air hit him. The darkness became a shroud. A stiff wind was up as he walked to the cliff's edge. The top of the breakers curled into ominous overhangs, breaking the symmetry of the waves below them. The wind tossed tiny fragments of cold spray into his face.

Something in his heart pounded, and something nameless clenched at his throat. He wanted to yell. Old emotions he'd buried didn't feel so hidden right now. He allowed himself to feel them. For the first time in forever.

He wanted to throw himself onto the grass, onto the sand. Beat his fists against terra firma. Why did nothing ever work out? He'd done what was asked of him. Ridded himself of his feelings. Tried to function like a normal human being. Made money.

The only place he hadn't been able to pack the fucking feelings in hard enough, to keep them from spilling out, was with Michael, who was now rotting somewhere in a South American makeshift prison in a hot, humid jungle.

Unwittingly, Nathan had split open Og's heart with one easy, uncalculated statement. Taken it and his soul-exerting power over him.

He doesn't even know me.

Og stood for long minutes. Hurting.

His mind on one track. The huge, unscalable barrier between him and the man he'd just fucked.

But he got a grip. Poet-boy thought this was about Og's investment. Un-fucking-believable. So much for being deep, empathic, and sensitive. Didn't he know that money wasn't the be-all and end-all? Sure, Og had played that game at the start, but that was good business—nothing more. They'd been through too much together in a short period of time, and then there was the kid, and Nate's mission. Og ran his hand over the top of his head. How the hell had life become so complicated?

Damn house. He wished he'd never come here.

He turned to look back at Manor House, so stalwart and solid underneath all the many restorations that needed to be done. The gold bricks, the clean lines of it, despite all the repairs that were still needed.

The bones of it were strong. Seemingly unbreakable, as if the house was trumpeting, unequivocally, that it was there to stay.

Off to the side, he suddenly caught movement. *Nathan.*

The rush of joy was quickly shut down by Og's gatekeeper: his brain.

Anger snarled in his throat.

Poet-boy didn't know who he was dealing with.

***

Nathan

Og met him like an opponent. For two men who had shared what they had, they were behaving like strangers.

Nathan looked at the ground, moved a tuft of grass with the side of his foot. "I'm sorry."

Outrage darkened Og's face, distorted it. "You don't even know what to be sorry for. You're pathetic."

The first blow.

Nathan took it, though it felt like it physically moved him back. He knew how to take crap like this. He'd done it many times before. His whole fucking life, in fact.

"I am really sorry." The words came out stronger, louder. Good thing, because the wind had picked up, creating a tiny din along with the rattling trees, loose shingles, and old shutters.

Og's expression constricted and Nathan read the pain in him. "What the hell are you sorry for?"

Feet planted shoulder width apart, Nathan answered, "I messed up."

"You damn well did. Here I do all this, commit to staying, help you and the kid, and... oh, you're clever." His expression turned savage, as if he'd been fooled. "You didn't say how you messed up."

"Because I don't know. You've told me how important business is to you from day one. How your whole life is riding on it for some reason. Not sure if you need to prove yourself still, as some kind of contender or what, but if you actually care—"

"*If* I care?" This time it was Og who moved back, as if struck. "What the hell does a man have to do? You, who claim to be so sensitive—you don't even see?"

"You're after the investment. Don't deny it. You're always on these secretive calls, talking about leaving. Did you think I can't hear?"

Og was his own man. Always would be. Even now, fighting in the moonlight for...he wasn't sure what... he knew that.

Nate watched as Og swallowed hard. Good. The arrow hit hard and buried deep. Nate hurled his words at the man he thought he loved. "You're a loner. You'll always be a loner. Nothing I do or say will ever change that."

Og snorted. "You say I'm a loner, and yet, if we really examine it, what part of your life have you shared with me?

Nate's breath came faster. "Me? Holy shit. I've shared everything with you. What's most important to me. My mission."

Og tossed it right back at him. "Oh, your mission. Your nameless mission. The thing anybody who takes ten minutes with you gets to hear about." Og leveled a dark look. "What have you shared with me about your past, especially that dark secret you call that locked room?"

A spasm ricocheted through Nathan. The studio was so important, so central to him, that he couldn't share it with anyone. Even that once Zach had been there was too much.

Irrational, sure. Nate knew the studio was the shrine to what could have been…what should have been.

The clouds shifted and rays of moonlight slashed across Og's face. Nate could really see his expression for the first time since their wild fight had begun.

Og's jaw was quivering, and there was a sheen in his eyes. He looked like a little boy. Like a man stripped bare, struggling to contain himself.

Nate knew what he had to do. "You think I don't care?" He threw the words at Og as if heaving a sheet of metal in his direction, uncaring if it sliced him in two. "Come on, then."

Without bothering to look back, Nate stalked off toward the house with every intention of taking Og up to the studio.

***

Og

Og wanted to tell Nathan to stop, to wait. To think this through. Og had never seen a man this upset. Once, a boxer who'd been fighting for his family—his wife and tiny baby were sick—wouldn't listen to him. Simply wouldn't listen. He'd tried to coach him, when the fight was spiraling out of control, to stop, to take a different tack. But no matter what Og said, the guy kept going back for more. Split lip, teeth missing, gash on his forehead, blood dripping, the sweat pouring off every inch of his body. He wouldn't give in, and he wouldn't stop until he lost the fight and the fight for his child's life. Then he stopped completely, all the way. It didn't end well.

Nathan had the same look.

Up the steps they trudged until Nathan stopped in front of the door in the wide hallway, his fingers tented on the knob. He looked down, held them there for interminable long moments, then he flung the door open and stepped aside.

The smell of old, undisturbed dust, fabric, linseed oil, wood, and paint hit Og. Dust moats moved silently. Nameless nomads barely existing in the slash of eerie moonlight from a high window. He felt rather than heard Nathan's silent reproof, the rejoinder in all his body movements and muscles telling Og to get the fuck in there. For once, he obeyed. Walked in, and stood in this great cathedral of lost dreams.

Rows and rows of canvases. Some stacked neatly, some haphazardly. The beginnings of color applied to the surfaces, others with graphite-sketched images taped to them. Landscapes, male love scenes by the score. The precursors, the harbingers, of masterpieces.

Electricity moved through him. The appeal of the paintings and sketches was immediate. Og had never studied art, had been to the Louvre once and had opted to leave early to go for coffee with a student, to put the make on him.

This place didn't stink of old people and still life. Nathan's work was the embodiment of being alive. Of brilliance and majesty from a soul that had been denied and knew what was out there for the taking.

Og gasped. "Nathan."

"I'm not talking to you. Walk around, see what you have to see, then get out."

Strangely, he didn't care. That was how elated Og was to be there in the presence of all this beauty.

One canvas held a moonlit night over heather and field. The moonlight suffusing the entire landscape so that each blade of grass was painted—no, drenched with silver luminescence. He could practically feel the cool air on his face, the magic of it. He wouldn't have been surprised if the blades had started a midnight dance, unearthly, yet joyous. Alive.

Alive. There was that word again.

In another painting, a river. The emerald tones of the encroaching forests barely parting to reveal its sparkling clarity. The life that was hovering right under the surface, ready to burst forth in joyous celebration, a warm promise.

He'd never seen anything like it.

And over there—*holy shit*. The painting almost rocked him off his feet. Half finished, the union of two male bodies. Passion, need, yet underneath it all, incredibly tender love culminating in—

He had to turn away.

It had to be his imagination that one man looked vaguely like him and the other like Nathan.

He turned around, aware he was leaving rows and rows of canvases untouched. Un-inspected.

He felt like he was in the den of Rembrandt. Or da Vinci.

"Nathan…"

"No. I said no talking. You're done looking, now get out."

Og searched Nathan's face, but saw there was no giving in on this one.

Whatever this man had been given to create this art, massive as it was, was far less than what had been stolen from him—scraped from his soul—to make him halt in mid-creation.

At the beginning of the genesis of it all.

***

Nathan

Nate watched as Og stumbled from the house, his face stone-like.

You've seen my soul now, damn you.

Nathan felt strangely naked. More naked than he'd been when they were making love, and it wasn't a feeling he liked. Worse, he knew with grim certainty that he'd never share his art with anyone else ever again. Every last canvas, every last brush and speck of paint had to go.

Perhaps he'd been waiting for this last viewer to permit this final release. He'd never go back to it. Not when it had been the ruination of his family and of his life.

***

Og

A half hour later, Og came upon Nathan sitting on a rock by the waves, looking out at the sea. Og had given him that half hour since emotions were running high, and people got stupid when they let their feelings fly.

Og wouldn't mind sharing the magnitude of emotion he'd been experiencing, ranging from reverence and awe to gratitude. Seeing such raw genius had humbled him.

He approached gingerly, then sat beside Nathan, who didn't flinch away. He risked placing his hand gently over Nathan's, which lay on his knee. Again, Nathan didn't pull away.

"Baby," he breathed softly, "that was you?"

A pause, then Nathan nodded.

"Nathan," Og whispered, "what are you doing heaving stone, digging foundations, and shoveling shit when these hands should be doing—"

Nathan pulled away, sharply hissing, "Like hell they should."

"I don't get it. You're obviously...talented isn't right. You're gifted. What gives?"

Nathan didn't look at Og when he ground out, "When your so-called gift ruins the lives of the people you love the most in the world, it's not a gift."

"What the hell are you talking about?" Og's voice was soft, but he couldn't keep the incredulity out of it. "How?"

Nathan still didn't meet his gaze. "My art was the most important thing in my life. They'd seen my talent since kindergarten, for shit's sake. There was even interest from New York—only a couple of gallery owners, but that was still a big deal. It was when the sexual overtones started surfacing, and in the wrongly decreed direction, that the small town we lived in went nuts. It isn't porn. It's love. But to them, it might as well have been."

Nathan held his hands together in a bloodless grip as he continued. "From the devil. Corrupter of youth. Shit like that. I was so cocky. I would do my art no matter what. They had to adjust because I had the right."

Og stayed silent.

"When my parents started losing money because patients started dropping off since they didn't want to go to the doctor whose son is a pervert, I wasn't so cocky anymore."

"You can't blame yourself for the stupidity of certain people."

"I didn't at first. I fought fire with fire. I put on a small show with the help of a few of the sane folks in town who appreciated me and my art and didn't give a fuck about my being gay. The show was well received. Some of the smaller papers did reviews, which were favorable, yet guarded. I was gearing up to do a second one, and then he came into my life."

Og's gaze narrowed. "He?"

"Elliot Overbrand." His voice dipped with the name.

Og's eyes narrowed, and he could feel his face constricting, his blood boiling, but he held back his anger. "Tell me."

"A journalist with questionable connections if you searched for it. I found a glimmer of them until the trail dried up. He had a vendetta. A homophobe who intends to ruin lives. Someone who relishes the power of it all, and I was the target. He came to our town and interviewed the assholes who were against me. He started publishing small pieces on the art scene, which he covers, and started raising questions about me, my character, and my view on kids." His face blanched. "So brilliantly done, subtly, but it was an attack. It was awful."

"On kids?" Og heard the horror in his voice. "You gotta be kidding."

Nathan's face was a frozen mask. "It heightened the attack on my parents. Suddenly, it wasn't only those few people that were boycotting Dad's practice, it was everyone, and it wasn't your garden variety homophobia. The question had been raised about my *preferences*, and my character had been tarnished. My folks took the brunt of it financially. They lost the house, and my dad lost a practice he'd built up. They were devastated."

"Your parents blamed you." Og was incensed.

"No," Nathan said firmly. "That's the crazy part. They supported me all the more. Told me I shouldn't stop my art or hide who I was. Dad started going on about all the great people in history who had the courage of their convictions. My room was littered with their biographies. And," his voice cracked, "they were so proud of me."

He stared at his hands, jaw set. "When their life savings was exhausted, they had to move into a shitty apartment building. Mom had to work split shifts doing breakfast and dinner prep at a diner to supplement their income. They're in their late sixties."

He shook his head. "They wouldn't take a dime from me. They wanted me to live my life and be my own man. Do them proud. They told me over and over, whatever I wanted to do, I would make them proud as long as I was me."

Nathan looked out over Refuge Bay, his gaze bleak and mournful. "That's when I gave up. My art died, and forget relationships with that track record." He gave Og a quick sidelong glance. "I managed, until you." He took another long look at his hands, then abruptly tore his gaze away. "Mistakes can be rectified."

Nathan seemed to steel himself for a moment, before saying roughly, "Take your stuff and go."

"Go?" Og gave a humorless laugh. "I don't think so."

"Well, you can—"

"I'm not leaving." He fixed his gaze on Nathan's drawn face. "And you know why."

Nathan raised his eyebrows but didn't say a word.

Perfect. Og leaned into him and kissed him.

Damn, there was no one like this man. His heart. His soul. Stupid poet-man who took the world onto his shoulders.

Og savored the moment when Nathan actually kissed back before tearing himself away.

"You take the whole universe on your shoulders, and you shouldn't."

Nathan blinked, sputtered. Apparently at a loss for words.

Og reached over and brushed the hair from Nathan's forehead. "You don't need to anymore. I'm here and I'm staying."

Nathan's voice dropped to a whisper. "Huh?"

"I'm Atlas." Og pointed at himself. "My new name where you're concerned."

"You're going to—"

"Yeah. I'm going to help. Take the burden off you. I'm going to sort this whole damn situation out ASAP. We're not going to sit back as if we've got no resources. We're lucky, you and I. We not only have resources between us, but we've got two big ones in the house. You know, those two people in the house who love you like crazy. Them. So, let's get in there and when they wake up, we're gonna lay it out, and then we're going to get this whole damn show on the road."

***

Nathan

They were all awake, though it was six-thirty in the morning. The windstorm had rattled loose a shutter, which was now flapping wildly, which woke Trasher. They'd all ended up together in the big kitchen.

Zach had thrown an overcoat over his robe, then gone out in the crazy wind to the little house, to Galen. He'd taken out meat pie along with sandwiches, added a container of fresh cream and another bottle of the precious wine, then came back quickly. Nathan was quite sure his ruddy cheeks weren't only from the biting wind.

Trasher was settled in the green overstuffed chair, a warm quilt tucked around her. Zach had tall, calf-high gray woolly socks on that did not go with his silk burgundy robe. He'd also donned a bright red woolen scarf against the ever-present drafts, wrapping it around his neck twice, leaving the ends to hang down in front, flapping.

Og had taken charge of the kitchen table, a big mug of coffee stationed in front of him. He had the air of a general, ready to jump into action at a moment.

Nathan stood at the sink, leaning against the counter. A motley crew, if there ever was one, but there was fire in this room.

"He's a pig. He's always been a pig, and now, he's even more of a pig. He's determined to destroy you." Zach roped the scarf around one more time and tucked it in. "I can't believe he's found you again. Apparently, ruining your life once was not enough. Bastard." Zach turned to Trasher. "Sorry, kid. But it's time for all-out war." Then to Nathan, Zach said, "You can't back down this time. We can't back down, no matter the cost."

"Easy for you to say. For us. But my parents...."

Zach's expression was grim. "Ask yourself, what exactly did they do all that sacrificing for if not so you could do your art, live your real life, and shine? Take the world by storm? What more can he do to them?"

"You really good at drawing and stuff?" Trasher asked. "I've seen your cartoons and stuff on things around here. You're really good at pictures, huh?"

"Honey, he was so damn good people were calling him the next wave of design. He's brilliant," Zach said. "He's got more talent in his little finger than most people do in their whole body."

"Kid, I'm not one for fancy-schmancy crap," Og added. "It took me ages to get one picture up on my office wall at the gym." Og glanced at Nathan wryly. "Usually, I'm partial to bulldogs, fedoras, and a good deck of cards." He circled his mug with his big hands. "But even I couldn't stop looking at his paintings. He's really good."

Og stared at Nathan meaningfully. "I say we put on a show. Right here in Refuge Bay. The biggest, most exclusive Nathan Gentael art show ever seen. No more hiding." He took a big gulp of his coffee and slammed down the mug. "Your art comes out of the closet, buddy. Like you. It's time to fight fire with fire."

Nathan's insides trembled. A show of his work. After all this time. Terrifying and enticing at the same time. Everything he'd ever dreamed of, or ruin?

But another picture hammered horribly in his head.

Fuck that. It'd already happened.

He hadn't been able to fight asshole Elliot before. Nate's reputation and his art had been shredded, and his parents had borne the brunt of what happened.

Nate's heart was in his throat when he glanced over at Og. The man was like a bull. Strong, massive. Immovable, and so damn determined. He'd said a lot of things outside that Nathan had a hard time believing.

"I know you're on board, Zach. You've always been on board, but between the two of us, I'm not sure what kind of an opposition we can mount. What kind of a show we can put on." His gaze flicked to the little imp in the big green chair, eyes wide. "There's Trasher to think about." Nathan looked at the child who lived in his heart. "I couldn't bear it if you were hurt in all this. I know he'll go after everyone I love."

Og was outraged. "You're talking, and I'm hearing the number two. What the hell—heck," he corrected in a growl, "am I?"

"You're a somewhat removed investor," Zach spoke to him, unruffled, flicking a stray fabric ball off his scarf. "With interests in a gym elsewhere. You spend a lot of time talking in private about who knows what, and who knows what you have going on in your life."

"My calls be damned." Og shoved the chair out from under him and went to the sink. He threw a quick glance Trasher's way, then stood beside Nathan and grabbed his hand. Nathan stared at him as he raised it, their hands entwined, clenched together, up high. Zach and Trasher stared too. "*This* is my life here. I'm here for the long haul. Whatever goes down, I'm part of it. Before and after." Og looked at Nathan. "That is, if you…." His voice suddenly went quiet. "If you…."

Nathan could barely swallow, but he managed a smile regardless of the pounding in his chest. "I do."

"Well, that's fine." Og rallied, then released his hand, wincing. "That's settled then." He narrowed his gaze at Trasher and Zach. "Time to haul ass."

Zach made stacks of pancakes and they'd eaten them with an embarrassingly huge amount of syrup. Trasher was dozing lightly in the armchair in a food coma while Og continued his arguments for a huge frontal attack. Zach was with him, but Nate was still uneasy.

"There's no way around it, man. We have to include the Refuge Bay community." Og's expression was steely.

"I'm with the boxer," Zach said. "Last time, that's what screwed you up. We need the few key members of the community on board to counteract the bullshit." Zach leaned forward, elbows on the table. "That's how that asshole works. He gets inside the community, stirs it up, and wins their support. All he needed was a few key members and their comments. It drove a stake through our hearts."

Nathan's gut roiled as he remembered, but it was too much. It felt incredible to have these wonderful people on his side, more than they'd ever know, but this was about launching exactly what Og had said it would be: a huge frontal attack against a determined foe. Sure, it was nothing but an art show, but Elliott Overbrand had made it more than that, and he'd made it ugly.

Nate didn't want to go through that again. He didn't want his parents to have to face that shit again, and he sure as hell wouldn't allow anything to touch Trasher. If this went south, so would making this house a refuge for men who needed it. Then Nate would have nothing left, and he couldn't handle that.

He cast his gaze down. "I can't do it again. If this falls flat, everything we have here is in jeopardy. Especially if we involve the community. This house, and why we want to fix it up, will be in jeopardy. We'd have to move, far away, for good. It's not worth the risk."

"Nathan." Og sounded desperate. "There's no way one man, especially not this Overbrand asshole, can affect your life in any real way again. Times have changed. He doesn't have the power you think he does. He can't hurt you anymore. Buck up, man."

Nate stared at Og and shook his head. "You don't know what it's like. You weren't in it. I know better."

Zach and Og looked defeated. For once, Og shut his big mouth, his expression defeated.

A little voice piped up. "Can I say something?" Apparently wide awake, Trasher said,

"So, this gooberhead wants you to run away." With her Darth Vader mug filled with hot chocolate she was alert and raring to go.

"He doesn't want me to have a life."

The weirdness struck him. Since when did he discuss his intimate business with a little kid? Surreal. His life had definitely slammed into surreal. An ex-boxer, a geek, and a little kid were the only team he had in the world right now.

"You mean like not getting to do what you want, not doing what makes you happy and not having fun, ever, that's what you mean?"

Nate's eyes widened, and he tilted his head. "Yeah, I guess so. Exactly that. That's what I mean."

"He's jealous of any fun you have."

"Kid's bang on," Og said, not even trying to mask his anger.

"How did you figure all that out?" Nate asked.

She shrugged. "S'not hard. That's what it's always like. In foster homes, on the street. People are always jealous. The bad ones, anyway. They want what you have, and if they can't have it," her voice dropped, "they take it away."

Her gaze fixed on him and he felt the stern rebuke in her suddenly wise, hazel eyes. "Are you going to let him take your painting and how happy you get when you draw something away from you? I've seen you," she added quickly and her eyes clouded with a child's judgment. "You're not going to let him take it all away from you and from us, are you?"

Shivers coursed through him, shot up and down his spine. Holy hell. The kid was right.

When even a little kid could see what was going on, he couldn't back down. It really was time to fight.

"No, Trasher," Nate said, looking at that sweet little face with the biggest, baddest grimace, directed right at him. "No. I'm not going to let him do that to me and to us."

Chapter Twenty

Nathan

Nathan worked like a demon. They'd opened the window in the studio. Seeing as it was a room over the addition, the ceilings were unusually high, and so was the octagonal window, but the light that came through was clear and bright. The breeze brought in much needed renewal. He was a man revived, crazy in his joy of it, and in his determination to create. He'd put on the best damn art show they'd ever seen in Refuge Bay and the surrounding area.

"You'll have to pick the pictures out. You have enough gay erotic art here to choke a horse." Zach scanned the pieces of art that were scattered everywhere.

"Mmmhmm."

"You have to choose a focal point for the exhibition." Zach rifled through the stack of canvases directly in front of him. "Holy shit. These are hot."

"You saw most of them years ago."

Zach's brows went up as a beatific smile filled his face. "That I did, buddy. That I did."

"Okay, well, stop getting off on them. There's work to do."

Zach leaned the stack against the wall. "Right. How can I help?"

Nathan took in his life's work to date, but his gaze stopped at the mound under the old, paint-splattered gray tarp.

He wasn't opening that baby up until he was all alone.

A thought struck him. "Quiche."

"What?"

131

"Don't mess with me. I happen to know you got an infusion of eggs from Nellie. Bill doddered over with them last night. I heard him."

"So?"

"So, get down there and make quiche. Make it by the freaking truckload. I want quiche for lunch, and so will the others. That's at least three. And by that I am including the new guy. He's crazy for your quiche, and possibly for a whole lot more. So, get on it. That's what will help me." He dropped his voice conspiratorially. "I need time alone."

Zach shook his head. "That will help you? Reckless amounts of quiche and alone time?"

"Yes."

"Fine." Zach dusted off his signature black jeans, then gave him a knowing look. "I'll be up in about an hour and a half then. Maybe two. And when I am, I'll knock on the door then leave your tray off to the left. I'll make sure it's hot and well covered. That work for you?"

Zach was the best friend anyone could have.

"That's exactly what I need. Keep Og away, and the kid. Molly too, at least for now."

Zach nodded firmly. "Done."

***

Nathan

Days later, the focal piece still eluded him.

Well after midnight, Nathan paced, the sea air wafting into the cold room, the sound of the waves crashing relentlessly in the background. He figured everyone in the house was sleeping, as he'd heard doors slamming and them going to the bathroom a few hours ago. Trasher had walked by his door earlier, right before her bedtime, and in a singsong voice had wished him good luck.

Actually, her exact words had been, "May the force be with you, doof." He'd smiled and his heart had warmed.

The reason he was holed up was to get the pieces for the show selected from his previous work, and none of it was falling into place. Especially the centerpiece, from which all the other pieces would flow. He still didn't know which one he wanted to use.

He'd scoured all the canvases, even taken brush to a few of them, added color. Fleshed in additional images, played with perspective, but nothing worked. Nothing said what he wanted it to say.

After the events of the last two years—the debacle with his parents and his own descent into depression, then getting the house, the miracle of meeting Og, and having little Trasher deposited in their laps—the subsequent richness and explosion of life that had ensued, it had a theme. He'd learned a lesson. A big one: trust. The emergence of life after death. That light follows darkness. All of it sang to him, came with a rhythm of its own, when he least expected it.

Life was good. What a wild thing to say when he'd been through so much pain, and likely would again, but it was good. Amazing, even. The biggest lesson of all, something he could scarcely put into words, something that was simple but powerful was going to be the theme of the entire exhibition. He'd keep that close to his heart.

The focal piece had to be perfect, but nothing was right.

A loud scratching at the door marred the midnight silence and made him jump. A soft woof sounded, and he smiled. Molly. Nellie and Bill didn't mind the dog visiting them, spreading love through the neighborhood. Zach had probably already called them, let them know she was settling in for the night.

Nate squatted, opened the door, and she rushed him, bowling him over onto the old floor, her big, gentle paws on his chest. She licked his face furiously, whined with joy as he stroked her. "I've been away from supper a few nights now, huh?"

More whines, louder. "Shhh, sweets. You'll wake Trasher."

Nathan chuckled as she licked up into his hairline, then sputtered. She moved off him, tail wagging, and they sat, snuggled up together against the wall with his arm around her, and looked at the mess of canvases he'd been working with.

"I don't know what to do, girl. This has to be perfect. That creep is gunning for me. He wants to make me out to be the biggest, baddest guy on earth. So much is riding on this." He ruffled her fur again. The softness of it soothed him momentarily, and he dug his fingers in deep, felt the warmth of her flesh. His muse, well before he had ever made a name for himself. "What picture should I pick? You tell me." Nothing but the panting as Molly cuddled up against him as he tried to make a decision.

They sat there for a while in companionable silence. Then, Molly turned from him, started nosing into a pile of papers on the floor, whined.

"What have you got there, girl?" He looked over, and there, in that long-forgotten list, were the names of all the men he was looking for to let them know they could come to the house. He'd brought it up here days ago as a sort of a talisman, then put it on the side for safekeeping, away from all the paint and turpentine.

If only they could have what he had now. Sure, there was still a lot of uncertainty about his situation: the art show and Overbrand, but he took everyday joy from small things, and the community. Some of the men he wanted to help had worked hard to get their lives together with some success, only to be relegated to more suffering.

Suddenly, it hit him: The simple things in life—the little things.

He leapt up, excited. He knew which paintings would work, would sing. Would frame the theme. He bent to hug the dog, who was looking at him askance. "Thank you, girl. You gave it to me. You told me. Don't look at me as though I'm nuts. You really did."

She jumped up, excited.

"Okay, so I know what the content is going to be, the sub-theme, but that damn focal piece…"

Molly trotted over to the one painting he'd shoved to the side, the one under the gray drop cloth. The one he'd studiously avoided. Molly pawed at it.

"That's the garbage pile."

She pawed at it more.

"The canvas is wrecked. There's a great big gash in it. I don't even want to tell you what was going down when I painted that one. When I…" He shuddered with the memory of it. "…slashed it."

She looked up at him with those dark eyes almost like the deep sage of Og's eyes.

Holy hell. It came to him. Damn. *I've got it.*

He patted the dog's head furiously. "You're the best, Molly. Let's go to the kitchen. I've got so much work to do, I better fuel up. There's a bit of turkey down there. When I fuel up, so do you."

She wagged her tail as if she knew she'd be getting food soon.

"Let's go, girl. I've got a shit-ton to paint."

***

Nathan

Five days later the work was done. Nathan sat on the old, uneven planked floor, wearing the same clothes he'd worn the morning he'd started.

He was exhausted but excited.

His eyes panned the row of canvases that were ready now. A few bits and pieces needed work still, but nothing more than the completing touches.

To think I would have burned all this. God.

The bones of the exhibit were done. He'd found paintings that were already mostly complete from that earlier period in his life and had finished them. Then he'd done more special, select studies to complement them, especially the main piece in the show, which was finished.

He leaned against the wall, grateful for its support. It seemed this place was still his cathedral of creation. Somehow, when he entered it with the right spirit, this room and this whole damn house gave him everything he needed. He owed another debt of gratitude to this crazy old place. It had shielded him and sheltered his art, held it waiting for him in this room while he ran off to find himself.

He stroked the sleek wood of the floor. He'd been struggling to find a new name for this beautiful, still half-broken-down building, for the mission that was being birthed right here, right now, with all these wonderful people close to him.

He would call it Hope House.

"Let me in. I wanna see," Trasher's insistent voice yelled from the other side of the door. "You've been in there forever."

He grinned. "Are you here with food?"

"I'm always here with food."

"Aww. Do you miss me?"

"I don't miss you. I need to discuss the menu with you." A pause. "There's been too much damn quiche."

He laughed, deciding to overlook the swearing. It continued to creep in often. "Liar. You always eat mine after you finish yours."

"Well, yours doesn't have green beans."

"Point taken."

"Are you coming out or not?"

"I'm coming out. I'll be downstairs in thirty." He paused. "You know I need a shower, right?"

"Ewwww." Then he heard the loud stomping of feet as she ran down the hallway and escaped down the long staircase, whooping and yelling.

The kid was theatrical. A drama princess.

His heart expanded, then panged.

He so wished she were his kid.

Chapter Twenty-One

Og

Og stood in the early morning sun on the side of the barn closest to the waves crashing nearby. It was weird how lost he'd felt without Nathan the last few days. There'd been work to do for his boss, Palmer, and Og had taken care of it, returning to New York, where he visited the gym, did a session with the guys. While he'd been happy to slip back into his old routine, something had been missing. He found himself itching to take the 'Stang out on the high road, back to the crazy little peninsula, to the house with a cherub and a flying pig on the chimney. He worried about Trasher and missed her quirky humor. He'd even missed Zach.

Og'd returned last night, and Nathan was still behind closed doors, painting up a storm. Og glanced back toward the house, eyeing the studio's window, and saw the glow of pale yellow emanating from it.

He couldn't wait for the show, for Nathan to unveil himself to the world again.

His body was strangely on fire. Sensitive, kind Nathan who was so powerful and didn't quite know it yet. Oh sure, he had flashes where he'd stand up for himself, but poet-boy still hadn't fully claimed the raw essence of who he was.

Og wanted to set Nathan's life straight, and help him grow into the man he could and should be. That bit was fierce, and Og marveled at the depth of his feelings for Nathan. He wanted to live with the guy, forever. Maybe some of Nathan's sensitivity would permeate Og's thick skull, his rawhide skin, and make him into more of a human.

He took another look up to the window, high above the addition. He wanted to stay out here in the cold where he could see the studio's light. He actually found himself pining for Nathan.

His phone vibrated, deep in his pocket.

"Reiden."

"Your brother's been moved."

He blinked. "Is that good news?"

"He's being transported through the jungle. My contacts don't know exactly where he is, but we're on it. We don't have much time because the conditions of transport are not optimal."

His throat was suddenly dry. "Meaning?"

"Your brother's hungry and ill. Barefoot. They're moving deeper into the jungle."

Terror radiated through him.

"What do we do?"

"My men are on it. In the meantime, say nothing to no one. We want Michael out of there alive, which means no one knows what's going on except you, me, and my team."

Og had money coming in now and he could afford the rescue effort as long as he skimped everywhere else.

The Watcher continued. "After we find him, we'll extract him."

Og was scared to hear the answer, but he had to ask. "How likely is it to be successful?"

"A million things can go wrong in the jungle. My men are pros. We're trained and ready, but nothing's guaranteed."

Og was strong, but his damn knees about buckled.

All he managed was a terse, "Thank you. Please find him and bring him home alive."

"That's the objective."

Silence.

Holy hell. Og was reeling. His phone vibrated again, making him jump. A quick glance alerted him to this caller. Jill in Palmer's office. He was met by her sultry voice, and managed to respond as normally as possible. "Hey."

"I need to tell you something."

"Shoot."

He heard her shuffling papers in the background. "I don't know what's going on, and it may be nothing, but I saw a file on Palmer's desk from when we interviewed for the position."

"And?" The word shot from him like an expletive.

"I looked in it when he was out. It's the form he used to interview all the applicants."

"Which means?"

"Well, it's unusual. He's fastidious. Once he's done with something, he puts everything away. It's one reason I don't have full access to his office. He does all his own filing, and knows where everything is. He shreds stuff he doesn't need anymore. If he's got those forms sitting on his desk...."

"You think he's looking for my replacement."

"It doesn't make sense. He's happy with you."

This couldn't happen. Not when Michael needed him even more than ever.

"You better make sure he isn't looking. We had a deal, and I'm not playing around. This is serious. You got that?"

"Don't threaten me. I've helped you, and I'll continue to help you. I'll do my best, but I'm warning you, Palmer's his own man. If he decides to hire someone else..."

"There's skin in the game for you too, don't forget."

She huffed. "I won't. Just make sure all your ducks are in a row because if he comes looking and finds something, you're out on your fine ass. I'm warning you. This is your heads-up. It may be nothing, but the file was there this morning. It had no business being there. You're welcome."

Dead air.

Shit. He needed that money to save his brother, who was being dragged deeper into the jungle while Og stood in an ocean mist.

"You coming inside?"

He turned at the sweet young voice. Trasher, in the baggy fleece shorts and too-long t-shirt they'd put on her for bed, stood a few feet before him. She looked like a tiny little gym-rat. "Zach says he's got coffee on and there's some for you."

He'd been so far away from this new life that he wanted so badly.

Could he make it all work, and still take care of Michael?

He had to. He'd never leave his kid brother flailing. If it took dying to find him, Og would. It was a decision he didn't take lightly. The thought of leaving Nathan killed.

Trasher and Zach too. He couldn't leave any of them.

They were all in his heart.

Which meant Og had to do both. Stay here and save Michael.

"Og?" She looked confused, unsure where he'd disappeared to.

He looked at her, a fidgeting little girl with wide eyes, and in his mind's eye saw Michael at that age. Looking to him. Wanting his attention, or to play, or seeking his big brother's guidance.

This little girl wasn't Michael. She was lost, and without a family. A child who was looking to him for help, and he'd pledged to be there for until she had to leave. He wished they could find a way to keep her forever.

"Hey, squirt." He moved toward her, ruffled her hair, his voice gentled. "Coffee sounds fantastic." He saw the hesitancy leave her. "Let's go in." He eyed her. "Later we'll go into town and get you something pretty to sleep in. One of those fancy shops where a nice lady will find you something fit for a princess."

The reassurance had the desired effect. A tiny smile spread, and she reached up her hand, held it there, as he smiled and grasped it, marveling at the soft flesh and the tiny fingers that curled around his.

Hand in hand, fists clasped together, they walked back to the tall, yellow-bricked house that was waiting to welcome them inside.

Chapter Twenty-Two

Nathan

Nathan stood outside the old country store and took it all in as if seeing it for the first time. The dusty wood painted blue-gray, the big storefront window crowded with items residents somewhat separated from the mainland would need. Set on a parcel that also housed the marina farther down, the store had been a focal point during his summers here. Gumballs. Ice cream. T-shirts. Bug spray.

Old memories wouldn't get him through now. He needed to walk in, reintroduce himself, talk about his art, and share that he was a gay man being harassed by a homophobic asshole. Not exactly the hey-how-do-you-do ice breaker he wanted to start with, but with Elliot on his new crusade, Nathan had to beat the bastard at his own game.

Og had wanted to come with, but Nathan had flat out refused. He'd never know who he was until he found his balls.

He sucked in a deep breath, pushed the door open, and walked inside.

The store's interior held a murky darkness, with ceiling fans of all different designs rotated at regular intervals above the aisles of goods. A few locals were milling about, browsing through typical vacation gear interspersed with household needs and the latest magazines.

"Can I help you?" a woman of ample girth called to him without looking at him from behind the wooden counter. She was busy unwrapping tiny metal fans from a big cardboard box, whipping off the bubble wrap with gusto. "Specials on the lunch counter are grilled cheese, homemade tomato soup, western omelet that's left over from breakfast, and tofu scramble. Left over from forever."

He gave a quick smile at the witticism, then cleared his throat. "Yes, excuse me. I wonder who I'd talk to about renting space for a show—an art show. I'd like to post something on the bulletin board or the window. Is that possible?"

The woman stopped, took a long look at him, and her face broke out in astonishment. "Nathan Gentael, *is that you?*"

He took a closer look. "Cleotha? Delight overtook him at seeing the original owner's daughter. "I thought you were long gone and living in the city."

Cleotha beamed. "I had. Made my fortune, then did what I wanted with it, which was to come back here. Mom and Dad are traveling, but they come back when they want to rest." She planted her hands on her hips and gave him another wide smile. "I heard tell you were back. Orval and Sundance were in here a couple of days ago, saying they saw Manor House with the chimney going, and said they saw you. They were pretty excited, let me tell you. One of our own back." She pinned him with a look. "You here for good?"

He waited a beat, unsure what to say. "Don't know right now, but I'd like to be. It's called Hope House now, by the way."

"Hope House? Intriguing." She grinned. "I'll remember that. We can sit and have a chat about it soon over at the lunch counter. When I'm not so dad-blasted busy."

He smiled. "Ah, what about the space rental? Where's there a decent space with good light?"

She openly ignored his question. "What's that?" She eyed the portfolio under his arm.

"Oh, this is what the rental's for." He laid the portfolio on the counter, opened it, and positioned it in front of her, heart in his throat. "Take a look."

She thumbed through the art, page after page. A few innocuous landscapes, then the portfolio quickly flowed into pictures of love. One man gazing at another, his soul in his eyes. Many more like it followed, becoming more graphic.

"You did these?" Her expression was focused, intent on the images.

"I did."

It seemed he waited about a zillion years until she finally spoke. "Honey, they're top-notch. The stuff I read about you was no lie.

Another thing." She raised her gaze to his face. "Seems like you know what you're painting about."

He swallowed. "I do."

She pursed her lips, nodded. "Maybe not everybody's onboard in Refuge Bay."

"I know." He cleared his throat. "But it's who I am."

Suddenly, the smile definitely reached her eyes. "Well, that's fine, Nate. You know, Sundance's barn needs some cleaning, but the light there works. What's more, it's in a spiritual reserve. I mean, he's always going on about that, but you walk in, and it does hit you. That work for you?"

Excitement bubbled, along with the relief he wished he didn't feel. She was all right with him and his art. "It does."

"Well, great." She bustled over to a wooden index file, pulled open a tiny drawer, and extracted a card. "Here's his contact. Give him a shout. He'll be happy to hear from you. Tell him I sent you. And Nathan?"

"Yeah?"

The look in her eyes was piercing. "Anybody got a problem with my old pal Nate, they got a problem with me."

***

Nathan

Nathan had a tense moment speaking to Jonas and Courtney until he realized they were both thrilled about his show and his reemergence into the art scene.

"It's about time, man. Your two previous shows rocked the art world, then you dropped out. It's time you spilled some of that Gentael fairy dust on the world again. Home's the best place to start."

"You're good with the catering I suggested?" Courtney replenished the cookies as they sat around the old farm table while baby Ammie played in her playpen, gnawing on her own soggy cookie. "Homemade farm-fresh cheeses with bread from Williams' bakery." She winked at Jonas. "Sam Tilson's first press will be way too late, but he's got a nice sampling of wine from a few months back. Would that do? It's local. I'm sure Julio said they still had some." She nodded at Nathan. "Let's hit Scott up for fresh honey. You remember Scott Graham? He's the local beekeeper. They do crazy things with it. Infuse it with flavors. Call it Funny Hunny. It's selling like crazy."

Nathan mentally added up the costs of all these amazing but likely premium goods. "It sounds amazing. I can't believe you're going to these lengths for me."

"Pfft. It's nothing. When hay baling comes around, I trust I'll see your skinny ass out there?"

The thought warmed him. He smiled at Courtney. "Absolutely."

Ammie started wailing, and Courtney disappeared with her.

Nathan winced. It was time. "So, man. I got something to clear up with you."

"Shoot."

"Listen." Hell, he was going to mess this up. "You know I'm gay, right?" The sick feeling swirled in his belly. "You know, right? I mean, I haven't advertised it but..." God. He was making a botch of this, but the picture of his parents in that little apartment with their life savings gone was all too real.

Jonas gave him a blank look, then spoke slowly. "Not sure if you knew, but Nate, old boy, I think I should inform you," he looked him dead in the eye, "I like cream in my coffee. Is that okay?"

What the hell? Dude lived on a farm. He could drink anything he liked. Literally. "Uh, yeah. Sure."

"Glad that's okay with you, but even if it wasn't, I don't think that really changes anything. Personal preferences, you know? That's all they are. They change nothing serious in my life, or anyone else's." He gave him a meaningful look. "You know what I'm saying?"

Relief suffused him. "I do, man. Thank you."

One of Jonas's farmhands, Ty Brewing, walked in and nodded at them. "'Morning."

"Hey, Ty. This is my buddy, Nathan Gentael. He's going to be putting on an art show out here on the peninsula, and we're all helping. Oh, by the way, Nathan is gay."

Nathan blinked. What the—?

He watched the slow smile spread over Ty's face. "Gotcha." He crossed to Nathan, shook his hand firmly. "I hear you're back for good. Prodigal son and all that."

A complete one-eighty from what he expected and had experienced before. Nathan was dizzy with the difference. "What was that all about? You gay, man?"

Ty shook his head. "Not last time I checked." He grinned. "I check regularly. Get the ladies to check, too."

"Gotta say," Nathan shook his head, "I wasn't expecting this."

Jonas shot a glance at Ty and nodded, obviously giving him the floor.

Ty said, "Man, I got better things to think about than what a guy does with his dick." He shrugged. "Your dick, your choice."

Nathan looked at Jonas. "This isn't how things went before. You know that."

Jonas reached for a pen and pad and settled in at the table. "Shit's changed. The world's a different place." He wrote something at the top of the notepad. "If I were you, I'd keep an eye on Orval Wainwright. He hates anything new, thinks we should all live in the past. Cuddle up to Edison. He's got some clout."

"Yep. I agree." Ty nodded at Jonas. "Okay, let's figure out how this is gonna work."

Nathan now had help to clean up the barn, if Sundance approved having the event there. Ty, Jonas, and a few others could be counted on. Nathan had Galen, Zach, and Og, who would be directing everyone within two minutes. A proper path would need to be laid leading to the barn. Ty suggested adding solar lights outside, a few minor refurbishments to the inside, some clean-up and landscaping around the barn would help.

After all his angst, to learn he had supporters gave Nathan hope. Orval Wainwright and his band of "yesteryear is better" folks were going to be a problem, but Nathan had help now. Nonetheless, he shared his worries.

"Don't worry, man. Ol' Orval's got other things to worry about. I saw him and Marnie Shulitzer in a hot and heavy conversation with some guy the other day." Jonas leaned back in his chair, tapped his fingers on the edge of the table.

"Yeah. Someone told me after, the mystery man was from New York. Newspaperman."

Nathan flinched. With all the support he'd been given, all the hope he'd started to feel as the day progressed, there it was. Things weren't as wonderful as he thought they might be. In fact, they were downright dangerous. Way more so than he'd envisioned when he started out this morning.

Elliot was out and about gathering his ammo.

Chapter Twenty-Three

Og

Nathan looked a little green. Og wondered how he could help set him at ease. Once Nathan had made his connection, things had progressed at a rapid pace. Two truckloads of people, some of whom Nathan remembered—farmers, artisans, shopkeepers— had descended on Sundance's barn during the weekend and cleaned it spotless. They'd hauled out old equipment, moved some of it to roped-off areas inside and out—for controlled ambiance, they said— then swept the floor and washed the windows, then fresh straw had been brought in. Tobias, the local electrician, had installed pot lights, and Courtney's team had gone crazy, putting up fairy lights everywhere they could think of: on the rough-hewn beams, on the old gnarled trees out front, along the edge of the old antique shop counter Jonas had dragged in with Ty as a reception area and bar. There were big metal bins behind it and a couple on the side to hold ice and the local beer, wine, and kombucha.

Barrels were set up as tables with wooden tops affixed. Wooden chairs, rescued from too many basements, barns, or the elements, had colorful, fancy pillows tied on them. A couple of graceful old couches had been carried in, and old throw rugs placed in front of them, creating conversation spaces. A hand-lettered, chalk sign inside mimicked the one outside where Og stood with Nathan.

Nathan Gentael—Unwrapped. Saturday night — 7 p.m. Refuge Bay.

Tonight.

The ads had been running for two weeks straight. When Nate's Aunt Tilley and Gram had been informed they got busy. Even though they'd been out of the art scene a while now, they'd done their best to drum up support for their boy.

After the barn had come together, Nathan had chosen the pieces he wanted to display, and Og, Galen, Jonas, and Ty had helped hang them.

"It's breathtaking." Og stood beside Nathan in the wide front entranceway they'd staged right inside the barn doors, taking it all in. Best part, Og had stood back when the community had taken over.

"It's happening tonight, lover." Og grabbed Nathan's hand and squeezed. "Don't forget, I'm here no matter what happens. If something goes south, we'll deal with it together. Shift it to north, babe. Together." Nathan smiled, and Og saw an inner light start to emanate from his man. "You excited, babe?"

Nathan strode around the barn, then grasped one of the huge supporting beams as he turned back to him. "This structure has been here for over two centuries. Housed the animals that kept people alive, and at one point, when the farmhouse burned down, it sheltered two families. They lived here in peace and safety until they were able to rebuild. When they did, they rebuilt more than that one house. They started this community."

Og nodded. "Yeah, Sundance told me." He looked up into the loft, perusing the large stocks of grain and feed that had been hauled up there for safekeeping during the show. He watched Nathan stare into the dark interior without moving his hand from the beam. Almost as if it was giving him support.

"Is this going to be my beginning or my end?" The words were so softly spoken that Og could barely hear them.

A shadowy figure appeared out of the dark, moved slowly and surely toward them. Almost a specter, his form took on shape as he moved into the shimmering light from the one string of fairy lights. "Sundance."

The handsome older Native American they'd met a couple of weeks ago appeared before them and nodded solemnly. "I came to see if you need help." He looked around. "The old place cleans up well, doesn't it?"

"I can't thank you enough," Nathan started, then looked down as Og squeezed his hand again. "We can't thank you enough."

"It is as it should be." Sundance scanned the barn from top to bottom, in one big arc. "Ahotasu is here."

"Ahotasu?"

"Beloved."

Nathan lowered his head. "Thank you."

Sundance gave him a thoughtful look. "You show the true grace and appreciative nature of a real man, and the courage that makes a man in spirit." He closed his eyes, bowed his head briefly. "I am honored to be in this with you and your partner." Then his face lit up in a grin. "After the show we'll party."

Something was off. Nathan looked out of sorts. Not for the first time, Og wished he knew what Nathan was thinking.

Hell. He could practically hear Nathan's saying: *If only it could be that easy. If only it wasn't, maybe, the end of everything...*

Og couldn't stand it any longer. "A moment, Sundance, okay?"

"As you wish." The man moved off toward the bar to check supplies.

Og pulled Nathan over. "Listen, love. If things do go south...." Nathan's eyes widened. "...we'll sort it out. It won't be that bad." Og watched him carefully, trying to impart strength.

"If everything hits the fan and I'm the biggest pariah on the face of the earth, if they strip everything from me and do even worse things to my parents and I have to watch all that go down again, will you..." He choked.

Og gripped his hand. "I will never leave you. I've learned my lesson, and I'm done drifting. It was never that much fun, and now I've found you and Trasher, I know where I belong. I'm here for the long haul, babe. Whatever happens, while I draw breath, you have one thing you can count on. I love you, and only you. I'm here, and I'm not going anywhere."

Og stared deep into Nathan's eyes, asking the question too. It floated in the air between them.

Nathan nodded, answering without hesitation. "Yes."

Og grabbed him and held him to his chest. He held him for a long time, and Nathan hugged him back. Hard.

Over by the bar, he heard the tinkle of glass as Sundance quietly sorted through the crazy variety of glassware the town ladies had hauled to the barn. None of it matched, but it was all perfect.

The show and whatever it brought was only a few hours away.

***

Nathan

From the minute they walked into the house to get ready, everything went wrong. "Where the hell is my shirt? The pants I pressed?"

Zach blinked and turned from the last-minute touches he was making to the light snack he'd insisted they all eat before the show. "What are you talking about? I laid it all out down here in the living room, like I told you." He pressed a finger to his forehead. "Ah, maybe it's upstairs, in your room, or maybe you or—" He gave Og a look. "—the behemoth moved it. Why don't you check before freakin' out?" Zach asked, and Trasher, who appeared looking little girl amazing in a pink, fluffy dream of a dress, laughed.

Og whistled. "Whoa, is that our Trasher?"

"Um, no." She looked down quickly, then up at him with shy yet bright eyes, her hands rubbing the soft fabric, as if she couldn't get enough. "For tonight, could I be…"

All three men stopped, frozen in place.

"Emily?"

They knew better than to make a fuss. "Of course," Zach said. "Emily, for one evening. You can be whoever you want."

Og said, "You can be Cleopatra, for all I care. Whatever you want." He ruffled her hair, then strode to the back door, making a hasty escape.

Even in the midst of all his pre-show jitters, which were more like pre-show earthquakes, Nathan knew this was a pivotal moment and had to be treated as such. It seemed that the little girl they all loved finally felt secure enough to reveal something she'd kept so secret from everyone—her real name.

His nervousness seemed inconsequential now.

He knelt down on one knee in front of her and stared into her uncharacteristically solemn face. During this last week she'd been getting less brash and more serious at times, as if a lot of important stuff was going on inside that hard-working brain of hers.

Nathan took both her hands into his. "Trasher, or Emily. Whatever you want, honey. It's all the same to us, because it's you, sweetness. We'll call you whatever you want. Whenever you want. It's your decision, always. Okay, sweetheart?"

When she threw herself into his arms, his heart sighed, and finally relaxed.

***

Nathan

Nate took the stairs two at a time. He had to get that damn outfit on. He'd leave off the jacket while they had the snack thing that Zach was determined to shove down their throats, nutritional freak that he was, and then he'd...

He came face-to-face with his closed bedroom door.

And there were a bunch of Zach's bags by one of the still-uninhabitable rooms. "Hey. I know I left my door open. And what's Zach's stuff doing up here?"

He threw the door open, started to bound in, and stopped short.

There, perched on the edge of his bed, sat his aunt Tilley, with the biggest grin he'd ever seen on her. She called to him in her strong yet heartwarming tone, "Honey bear."

"Darling." Gramma Ellesmere attempted a shout, but as she didn't have a lot of strength due to a cold, and it came out as an intense whisper. "We couldn't wait 'til that nasty addition was done. We had to come and see your show. What would your debut be without family?"

His heart expanded and his nose tingled as he tucked the logistics of where they'd stay out of his mind. Practicalities be damned. He loved these two crazy, ancient, turn-the-world-on-its-ear women. They couldn't have come at a better time. "Indeed," he said, and threw his arms around his aunt. "What would anything be without family?"

Tilley grabbed him and vise-gripped him into one of her famous, *sumo wrestlers are wimps* hugs. "Were you looking for that awful-looking outfit you were supposedly going to try to wear for your debut?"

He tried to yank himself out of the hug but gave in quickly. He adopted his strategy of counting to ten, then pulled himself out. By then she used up most of her energy on the hug. "I was. I need it fast. Do you know where..."

Then his eyes lit on the elegant, deep brown tux and vanilla crème shirt with a rainbow cummerbund hung underneath the old light on the wall. Stylishly cut, he could see the label and knew it came from a New York store. He'd never have been able to afford it, even as a rental. Drawn by its beauty, he stood in front of it and ran his fingers down the supple yet light fabric.

He turned to Gram, and she smiled. "For you, honey bear."

He flicked a glance at Auntie and caught her beam as well. "And honey, about your show. We made sure a few of the art scene reporters in New York, New England, and D.C. knew about it. They got directions on how to get here to your little barn, and on your background."

His eyes widened. "You... you?"

Aunt Tilley smiled. "We did."

He was totally flustered. The stakes had suddenly gotten a whole lot higher. He gulped. "Thank you so much."

"Good, good. That's settled." Aunt Tilley got up from the bed, took Gram's hand, and helped her up off the chair. "We wanted to surprise you, honey, but we're going to go downstairs now so you can get ready. I'm going to help that lovely friend of yours, Zach, with the food. He is lovely, but he doesn't know how to put together sandwiches. At all. I'll make sure things are done right." She would, and she'd drive Zach crazy in the bargain.

"Auntie, Gram, I'm so, so glad you came."

"We are too, honey bear. We hear there's a new man for us to meet?" She smiled. "We'll give him a good Gentael welcome, you can count on that. Finally, a man of your own. Good for you. And by the way, don't worry about us. We plan on staying a while, and we're going to be just fine. We can sleep anywhere. In an old room, in the kitchen. On the floor. Absolutely anywhere." She inclined her head toward him, conspiratorially. "Only not up here, love. Gram could barely get up the stairs."

Gram nodded her agreement wildly. "We won't put you out, honey. We'll be unnoticeable. We'll settle in fine. Anywhere," she said again and leaned close to him. "I need to be close to a bathroom, though. Midnight rumblings. Other than that, anywhere. All right?"

Nathan shook his head. They wouldn't be unnoticeable. They'd be the exact opposite. And he couldn't wait.

"I wouldn't have it any other way."

Chapter Twenty-Four

Og

Og stood outside, trying to collect himself. A bloody damn new thing for him. Not overly welcome.

"Hey." Galen strode by, in jeans and dark T-shirt covered in dust, obviously fresh from another session with the cottage. Bashing down drywall or some crazy thing. No one was quite sure which of them was winning. But they'd all seen the signs of progress around the place, and had decided to give him free reign, within reason. He still wasn't joining them at mealtime, despite having been invited. Though he'd still been amazing, helping out at the barn, and had morphed into a bit of a foreman when the pathway had been laid down.

Any other time, Og would be giving him a second look. But now nothing. No interest. None at all. "Hey."

Galen stopped, eyed him. "You need a hand with anything?"

"I'm good. Carry on." The words slipped out nonchalantly, but inside, his heart was hammering from nerves for Nathan. Galen searched Og's face for a split second longer, then looked away, and carried on.

Phew. Glad Galen left, Og needed alone time. He'd barely been able to get through that scene with Trasher. To think that sweet little girl trusted them enough to... He gulped down the emotion, squeezed back the tears. She was coming into her own.

Almost as much as Nathan.

It'd been amazing to see Nathan with his family. The way they doted on him, he was the center of their universe. It was all choking Og up too much. The whole family thing. After his own wretched early start in life, it was a miracle to have those old ladies embracing him like he was their family too.

Two things had to happen for Og to be truly happy: Michael had to come home safe, and Og and Nathan got to keep Trasher.

What started out as a deep dark secret had now become a millstone around Og's neck. He wanted to tell Nathan about Michael despite what the Watcher had said. They were getting too damn close to have secrets of this magnitude between them.

First, though, he had to get through tonight.

They'd discussed that if Overbrand showed up tonight saying he was a journalist they'd let him in. Other journalists were coming too, the ladies had apparently made sure of that, and it would make too much of a scene, create the wrong kind of news. They couldn't hurt Nathan's chances or his reputation like that. Not again.

But, oh boy, Og was going to keep an eye on that asshole, if he had the nerve to show. He'd have the kind of shadow he couldn't shake. Nothing would keep Og from protecting Nathan tonight.

He heard more laughter coming from the kitchen, and he couldn't wait to go back in.

***

Og

"Let's go." Trasher pulled at Zach's hand. "It's ti-ime. We'll be late. We can't be late. Let's go."

"Listen to the child," Aunt Tilley interjected, over at the kitchen sink. "She's got a good head on her shoulders, that one."

Both old ladies had adopted Trasher, who'd introduced herself to them as Emily.

Zach smiled. "Listen Tra—ah, Emily, we won't be late. We have to be there by six. And Nathan's not even down yet." Zach turned and let out a breathy, "Oh."

Og moved as Nathan strode into the room. Og'd never had butterflies in his entire life. Damn things were beating the shit out of the inside of his stomach right now though.

Damn. His man looked *good* in a tux.

His wavy brown hair tickled the collar and was swept back from his glowing face. Nathan was happy. Even facing a potential shit-storm, he was grounded, and seemed to know what he was about.

Poet-man was breathtaking.

Longing spread through Og's body as an odd thought snaked through him. If Nathan didn't need him to be a hero, then who the hell was he?

Nathan caught Og's eye and smiled. Those warm spicy eyes looked deep into Og's, and his heart tumbled. Hell. He felt like their hearts had connected in that split second.

"Let's go, let's go, let's go." Trasher caught hold of Nathan's hand and yanked.

Og's heart stuttered, and he stole one more quick glance at Nathan.

Duty called, and he knew it. Og turned, ready to walk out the door to this important night, with the family he was crazy about, bent on supporting the man he loved in his artistic debut. One that could fall flat, if the art scene so decreed, or, if that creep tried to hurt him, supporting Nathan in the maelstrom his life would become Og's primary job.

***

Nathan

The barn was aglow. The collection of paintings Nathan had selected to show were hung where he'd stipulated. He walked around one last time alone, the only one inside before the show started in twenty minutes, checking on everything.

The pot lights were down low, and fairy lights twinkled everywhere.

The make-or-break art show was about to begin, and he was ready. On some level, he'd always been ready. Maybe he always knew deep inside that his whole life was pushing him toward the one moment when it would all come down to fate.

The only thing hanging over his head was how failure would affect his family. They'd suffered and lost too much because of him. If for no one else but them, he hoped tonight reached some level of success.

Hope House would go on, but it would be a damn sight better if Nathan didn't have a cloud hanging over his head. Zach, Og, his auntie, and Gram were his family. He hoped Trasher…Emily would be there with them too. Knowing how cosseted he felt from having a familial embrace, he was all the more determined to ensure that others had a place to recuperate, to catch their breath, heal and have hope.

Three months ago, if anyone would've told him he would have Og standing strong at his back, Nathan would've laughed. Now he couldn't imagine his life without him.

He'd heard Og out front talking, but now he couldn't hear him. The fear he'd been pushing down for the whole last week that he thought he'd succeeded in conquering swept through him.

Where's Og? He couldn't do this without Og. He ran off to find the man who had become his unmovable rock. A necessity, like the blood in his veins.

He needed his Og.

Chapter Twenty-Five

Og

The cool night air shifted past him, but it did nothing about the sweat that now coated Og's body. He leaned against the broad expense of the barn, trying to stop the swirling.

"I'm telling you, Og, this is an order from Palmer. He's saying you have to come in right now, tonight, and be here by eleven thirty, if you want to keep your job. He's leaving on his plane at midnight and if you want to keep your job, you have to divest all your investments from the Manor House charity and halt all association with it. He doesn't want you within five hundred feet of the place. He wants you off the peninsula, and he's thinking of putting you in a different division. Relocating you." Jill was speaking clearly, but he could sense a frantic energy below her tone.

"He read everything I gave him about the place. Full background. What the hell happened?"

"He read something about it that was definitely off character for our organization."

"Off character? What the hell are you talking about? Nobody cares about this place. It's not even up and running yet. What did he read?"

He heard the shuffling of paper and the catch in her breath. "Here it is. Gotcha, you slimy little bastard. It's an article by some guy named Overbrand."

The breath shot from Og as he swiped his wet forehead. He'd pooh-poohed Overbrand's possible influence on Nathan's life the last few weeks. Told Nathan over and over that he could take whatever the man might do to his life, but first and foremost he had to be true to himself.

Og never thought the scumbag would affect his life.

The Watcher had updated him an hour ago that Michael had been given a death sentence for not cooperating, and the sentence was due to be served on a special holiday coming up in a month and a half. The Watcher needed two more weeks to ensure the intel was correct, then the extraction would take place.

Og had known he could afford it, had pledged the payment. But if Palmer kicked him out on his ass…

"I can't leave here. I owe him." Desperation made him blurt out the words. Fuck it, he couldn't tell Jill he loved Nathan.

"How can you pay him back without a job?"

"I don't mean that way. I mean…*shit.*"

He heard the shock in her voice. "You mean love. Og." Her voice lowered as she realized the full breadth of what he wasn't saying. "You love the guy, and you've pulled that whole protector shit on him too, I bet."

He felt weak. So weak. "Help me out here, Jill."

An army general would have been proud to have the command in tone and inflection she used. "If you continue your association with that guy, Palmer'll cut you off. He'll crush your balls, and your ass is out and gone. There are no second chances. He'll blackball you, Og. You hear me?"

Dammit. He knew she was right. Michael needed a second chance, desperately.

"You know what you have to do with no explanation. You can't tell him why. Palmer won't suffer his business being broadcast to anyone who's outside the circle of the immediate people involved. Do it."

A ragged breath tore from him, and he hung up without another word between them.

He knew what he had to do, no matter what it cost him.

He had to hurt the man he loved and destroy the life he'd miraculously been given, the biggest gift ever. The only real life he'd ever been offered.

He had to leave now.

Og reached into his pocket. His hand had stopped shaking through sheer force of will. He couldn't find anything to write on.

All he had was today's stock market pages, courtesy of his daily run to Cleotha's store. "Shit. Where am I gonna—" All he had was the bloody margin of the newspaper. He grabbed his pen, laid the paper against the weathered side of the barn, and wrote the note. He'd find Zach, press it into his hand, curl his fingers around it, then run.

Something he'd never done his entire life.

Then he'd descend into the cesspool he'd come from with no genuine, decent emotion left to him ever again.

He didn't deserve it.

The pain of knowing he'd abandoned not only the one man he'd ever loved, but also the little girl who had decided, against all that she'd ever learned and experienced, to trust him.

If Og didn't do this, he'd be killing his brother.

He went off to find Zach.

***

Nathan

Nathan caught sight of Zach and ran to him. A few members of the community were milling about, already there to help. He waved at Jonas, beamed at Cleotha, then turned his attention back to Zach. "You seen Og? I know I'm panicking, but I need to see him. I'm feeling a bit nuts. I'm sure I'll be fine if Og and I can talk or at least…"

Zach gripped him by the arm and yanked him behind a copse of trees. Then he stared at him, a helpless expression on his face.

"What?"

"Buddy. Brace. Og's gone."

"He's what? Did we run out of supplies, or did something crazy come up?" He was confused. "When will he be back?"

"Sweetie, he's not coming back."

Panic made his legs shake. "What do you mean he's not coming back?"

"Nate, he's gone. For good. He said he's sorry, but he couldn't maintain his obligations here." Zach pushed a crumpled piece of paper into Nathan's shaking hand. "He left you a note."

Nathan could barely focus, but he made himself do it.

With each word all the hopes he had that this was some kind of weird nightmare evaporated.

Og was gone and he wasn't coming back.

A gut punch like nothing he'd ever felt. He couldn't breathe. He couldn't—

"Hey, Nate. You ready for your big debut? We're all here for you, you know." Cleotha ambled toward him, beaming at him. "Mom and Dad might be by, too. They said they couldn't miss your show."

"Thanks, Cleo," he mumbled and managed a cursory wave, his mind racing.

Og had been tasked with opening the doors, making the announcements.

Only now, he wasn't here. For any of it.

I found him, after long last. After forever. We fit. We fit so damn good, exactly as we both are. Am I supposed to go on as if nothing has happened?

Hell. He couldn't do it. He was going to fold right here, right now.

"Nathan. Are you okay?"

The little voice cut through the miasma, through the shock. He looked down, and there was Trasher—Emily, looking at him. Worried and insecure. Her bottom lip quivered.

Ah, hell.

Something in him stiffened. A little of his missing strength coursed back into him. If he had to do this alone, he would. For the kid, and for himself.

"Buddy." This from Jonas, on the other side of the walkway, from over by the little solar lights Galen had put down to mark the path in the dark. "It's time."

A small crowd had formed on the footpath they'd created and put down so painstakingly, finishing it only a few days ago. *Him and Og.* When they'd been a family.

Shit happens. No matter if you're cut off at the knees and the stumps are bloody, raw, life goes on.

Nathan would damn well make sure it went on. He was going to do this like the man he was. Right here and right now. No matter what anyone else did.

"Welcome, everyone, to rustic Refuge Bay. The show is called Nathan Gentael Unwrapped. I hope you love it as much as I did creating these works of art. Ladies and gentlemen, I welcome you to my show."

The lights shimmered, and Zach opened the doors wide.

Chapter Twenty-Six

Og

Og sat in the tenth-floor, corner office, double suite that was meager by Palmer's standards. It was done in mahogany and teak, with plush oriental carpets, imported from a tiny shop in the backstreets of Morocco. The massive desk—in Palmer's world, the size of the desk equaled the size of one of a man's appendages—took up the center spot in front of the huge walls of windows.

The view was not New York City. Og had been summoned to Baltimore, as it turned out, and could have stayed with Nathan through the show. Instead, he was looking at the Inner Harbor where the sky showcased the shining moon and a thousand stars.

Over the working fireplace, Palmer's power portrait glared past him to the double-coated, bulletproof glass. His aura was thick in the room. It was as if he even commanded the elements, the great blazing orb in the sky, now descending into the gray ocean waves below.

Palmer Tucker. One of the ten wealthiest men on the eastern seaboard who was keeping Og waiting. He'd been summoned to be there, to drop everything and leave his life behind, but Palmer was nowhere to be found. Which had to be all right since he held the power. The man held everything in his perfectly manicured hands.

Finally, the shithead swept into the room.

"Good. You're here." Palmer eyed the vellum notepad sitting perfectly centered in front of him, the Tibaldi Spartacus pen on top, his personal icon. "I'll get right to the point. As you know, you're not part of the Arrow portfolio anymore. You and that charity are done." He leaned back in the massive chair and steepled his fingers, not looking at Og. "I'm putting you in charge of the watchdog portion of Daiquiri Denizens. You leave in three days. Questions?"

Og's resentment flared.

Palmer continued, unconcerned. "I expect you'll want to be briefed. Jill or Otis will give you the pertinent information, and I've had this prepared for you." He pulled a file from under the notepad. "In here you'll find—"

"Just a damn minute."

Palmer cocked his head, clearly surprised.

Now or never. "What's wrong with Manor House?"

The answer came at him, full force. "One." Palmer extracted a batch of papers from another file. "It's barely a charity. I understand it's been registered recently, but it smacks of self-interest. Anything that hasn't been registered for two years, at least over one year, does not qualify for Palmer Industries. The image is wrong, and it can't be proven that it wasn't done to prop up someone's poor investments or need for money."

Palmer's face tightened and his eyes narrowed. "Two. I'm not satisfied with the work that's been done around there. I had that checked into also. Are you aware nothing's been done for at least three weeks? Except for the nonsense you participated in?"

Since the man thought he knew everything that was going on, Og wanted him to have it all. "There have been other priorities pursuant to the house's mission."

"Such as?"

"There's a little girl in residence, a runaway who was a battered child. She's required time, it's a delicate situation, and progress has been made. That's in alignment with the charity's focus on caring for the brokenhearted, though it was not seen at the beginning it would include a seven-year-old girl."

Palmer nodded. The muscles on his face eased for a flash, then constricted again. "And?"

This would be a harder sell. "The owner is an artist who had been up and coming, but dropped out of the art scene." Og silently offered up a plea for Nathan to forgive him for this next bit. "You could say he was the original broken bird, and lived his life that way until only recently." *Yeah. Until I showed up.*

That wasn't entirely true. Nathan had his mission set before Og had shown up, and was continuing it without Og. "He's recently revived the artistic side of his life. It was a difficult decision, but with success he brings more notice to Manor House—now renamed Hope House—as well as garnering more funding. That has taken the rest of the time."

"An uncertain business decision at best."

"It is. But one he was compelled to make. Hiding one's self never brings good. Instead it obliterates one's strength of character. Nor does it further the cause of true charity, not in the long run. It's directly contrary to it."

Palmer's lips pursed momentarily and his frame tensed. However slightly, but it was there. "So, now you're a psychologist?" He snorted, and in it Og read a cool derision. "The ex-boxer turned counselor?"

"I'm not, and don't claim to be. I'm trying to make the case for the other priorities. I've been there, involved in its daily running. I've seen it firsthand. Until the show happened—which took place tonight, by the way," he felt sick as he said that, but continued, "work was continuing. I did much of it myself, without compensation, and the work is one hundred percent sound."

"Making the case for it being charitable. Contributing your time."

"Yes."

"Well, I'm glad to see you've thought it out and can answer for your actions and decisions. Regardless, with articles like this hitting the industry rags, I'm distancing Palmer Industries and you from it."

"Articles?" Og felt the bile creep up his throat.

Palmer unsheathed a clipping from the heap of pages. "Here." There was the expected byline.

It only took a few moments to scan the untruths that reeked from the narrative. The facts could not be faulted, but the spin on those facts was vicious.

If this was what Overbrand was doing to Nathan tonight while Og sat there in plush leather chairs playing with millions of dollars... Suddenly, clarity descended on him.

He'd been so all fired, focused on Michael, and now he realized why. He'd never gotten over the shame he felt. He'd abandoned the kid, way back. Hadn't been there for him when Michael needed him. They'd been forced to adjust to the new circumstances without parents, and needed each other so badly. But Og hadn't been there, and he knew deep in his heart that had led to this awful, untenable situation.

What he'd done once again showed he hadn't fuckin' learned. He'd abandoned another person who depended on him. Whom he *loved.*

The import of it all sickened him.

He'd sold his soul in a crazy effort to obliterate his past sins. To make it all right again, with all the crazy crisscrossing of intentions, but to accomplish that, he'd abandoned someone else in their time of need.

The image of Michael languishing in that South American jungle eviscerated Og. But two wrongs did not make a right and sure as hell didn't fix his past sins. There had to be another way.

There was going to be another way.

Og stared at Palmer, hating him in this moment almost as much Og hated himself. He was the antithesis of everything Og aspired for in this new life he was crafting. One with new principles. Palmer manipulated people to do what he wanted without conscience or concern.

And how was Og better? For all his big talk, for all his bullish ways and the constant crowing about how he was beholden to no man, the way he strutted around, he too had manipulated people. Sure, on a smaller scale, but he was no different than Palmer in that regard.

Now, Og was a pawn, and he didn't like that shit at all.

Buck up. Be a man. Hadn't Og said those words to Nathan countless times over the last few weeks? Og had felt as if he were tutoring him, teaching him to become bigger, to take up more space on the planet. To be a *real* man.

Then how quickly he'd abandoned the man. Cowering, leaving everything he loved and had sworn he was committed to because another man snapped his fingers and demanded it.

Who was being a man tonight?

Og had left Nathan to face the biggest challenge of his life without so much as a word. Og had been holding the rope as Nathan dangled off a cliff, then simply thrown the rope over the edge and taken off and said, "See you later, buddy. You're on your own now."

Og rose. "Palmer, I've appreciated working for you. It's been hard at times, but I've achieved the objectives you set out for me.

More than that, to this day, I've respected you. I know business, but you're legendary, with good reason. I don't want to lose my job working for you."

Palmer sat. Expressionless.

"But I'm not abandoning Hope House *or* Nathan Gentael. I'm not going to divest my interests there. In fact, once you board your plane, I'm headed back there."

Og drew in a steadying breath. "I made a promise to a good man, someone without any agenda except to revive the broken spirit in other humans and help them to get back on their feet. I'm not going to break that promise. Not for you, or for the generous paycheck you deposit into my account, and for what it can buy me." *Michael.* "If you want, I'll look for another way to fund it, to get it considered a charity, without my trust. I can try to do that, but it's a long shot. If it comes down to leaving them without funds or help, I'm not pulling out of it. If that doesn't suit you, I respect either choice. If it doesn't, we best consider how we're going to part."

He thought Palmer would blink, but the impassiveness said business first above everything else. "Resigning is standard." He shrugged. "Then we're done. You can find another way to fund your lifestyle, if you're not going to live up to your obligations."

"Accepted. One thing you should know." *Michael deserved this much.*

"What's that?" Palmer slid a couple of papers into the file. He was already doing the tidying up Jill had said was his process at the end of a negotiation.

"I'm not funding a lifestyle. The most money I've blown the last month is on buying a little girl who's lived on the street for months three nighties, and a pretty pink party dress for the show tonight so she could look like a princess."

Palmer's brows winged upward a fraction.

"The rest is going to try to save a member of my family. I abandoned him when he was young, and he fell in with a bad crowd. I need to bring him home. He's alone on another continent, at the mercy of drug dealers." His voice broke for an instant, the emotion thundering through him. When he spoke again, he didn't have the power to project, so it came out in a low, stark tone. "I have to bring my boy home."

Palmer stopped filing, his hand in mid-air. "Your boy?"

"Figure of speech. My brother. Might as well have been my boy, with the start we had. All my pay has been going to that. Every penny. I gave up my apartment to fund it months ago in favor of a room over the gym, and I'm not paying rent now at Hope House."

Hope House had been sheltering him.

Palmer nodded, almost imperceptibly. "So, that's what's been going on. I assumed it was a sexual thing."

Og finally allowed a snide laugh. "No. Not the way you think. It's a love thing, if you must know." It shocked him he was saying the words. "A forever, 'til death do us part thing. I'm on my way back, if he'll have me. I'll take whatever package you give me— you're always generous—and apply it to Michael's rescue. If there's no package ensuing, I hope my partner and I can find a way to raise those thousands of dollars to bring my kid brother home. I hired the best because he needs the best, and Michael deserves it."

Og's exhaustion was creeping in, and there was nothing left to say.

With Palmer staring gaping holes into his retreating back, Og stalked out of the office and away from the only solid income he'd ever known.

Chapter Twenty-Seven

Nathan

The show was dazzling, with a wondrous energy percolating. Visitors milled about, talking about the paintings, pointing and nodding their heads in deep conversation. The bar area was doing a brisk business, and attendees reclined on the couches, munching the hors d'oeuvres and drinking the donated wine. There were more people than they could've expected, many from the mainland.

So far, so good.

Nathan knew better than to bask in the glow. Things could turn on a dime. Especially with Overbrand in the house.

Nate had kept a stiff upper lip through the whole show. He'd tried to force himself into the moment, even though a screaming voice inside of him kept yelling to be noticed.

He's not here. He promised to be here as I faced all this, but he's not.

He left and he's never coming back.

The pain was intense, but Nate had buried his feelings for years. He could cope without falling apart. He moved around the show, a shadow of a smile pasted on his face, watching reactions. That had given him some pleasure, knowing people were enjoying his work.

He moved to a corner of the barn that was shrouded in darkness. The setup committee had placed a chair there beside a rustic old table that had been hammered together in days gone by. The fat black nail heads still showed on the side, the wood, a deep grainy brown, worn by decades of use.

To the side, the old wooden framed window let in a slash of moonlight.

He allowed himself to sink into the chair, onto the fancy cushion, to take respite for a moment. His gaze lit on the leaflet that didn't look like his brochure on the table. He picked it up, moved the notepaper clipped to the cover. Underneath it, the headline read:

Gentael, a Vicious Fraud. His Covert Activities and His Latest Escapade—Desecrating a Runaway Child—UNWRAPPED.

He could barely swallow for a long moment.

To say it was unsettling reading a list of the things you'd done and lived for the last decade out there for everyone to read, as if you were a reality show participant, was an understatement. Their choice of words used to describe those things could uplift and inspire and make one look like a saint or make you look like a loser, a freak who didn't know what they were doing: a horrible, vicious, miscreant. An abuser.

The lies Overbrand told were horrific: *A young innocent corrupted. Gentael, this month, kept a young girl imprisoned for days before alerting the authorities. She had been kept in that ugly old mansion, away from the community, forced to pander to the disgusting sexual appetites of three vile adult males…*

Nathan was going to black out. Fractal images danced in front of his eyes, pale kaleidoscopes, phasing in and out over the reality of the barn, the show, and where he was.

There was no oxygen. He was fading.

Then he heard it. The whimpers, familiar ones, coming from one of the stalls nearby.

He blinked his eyes wide open. He was back at the show, the noises from the exhibition gallery intruding.

There was that sound was again. No doubt.

He leapt from his chair and strode past the thick rope stretched across the darkened pathway dissecting the two rows of stalls, ignoring the PRIVATE sign he'd hung himself earlier.

It took no time to find her. The sight turned him sick.

It was the same type of area they'd originally found her in all those weeks ago, abandoned and all on her own. The little girl whose soul, outrage, and sweet laughter had wound itself around all their hearts was in the stall, on the floor amid the hay, clutching an old dirty coat, her arms circled around it.

He was so shocked, he called to her as he bent toward her. "Trasher?"

She looked up, the moonlight coming in through the slats illuminating her face. She'd been so clean and so utterly presentable when they'd started the evening. Now, she'd reverted to the pre-Hope House girl. The scrubbed face was gone. Dirt marred her pretty cheeks. The ribbon was gone and her hair was matted where she'd burrowed into the straw to escape.

Worst of all, that pretty, pink dress she'd pirouetted in and treated like it had floated down out of the heavens as a miracle gift for her was a mess. Dirty, with caked-on mud and who knew what else, being as it had been a working barn not that long ago. A portion of the pink chiffon was torn from the hem she'd so carefully run her fingers around earlier in such delight.

Not to mention the tears that streaked her face, through the mud.

"Trasher, dear god. Are you—"

She shrunk from him.

Shocked, he stopped. "Honey, are you... are you *scared* of me?"

His worst fears were confirmed. "They say you want to hurt me. Billy said it's how you always do it to little kids. You do good things for a while and then you..." The rest was lost as the sob choked the sound and killed it.

He picked out the balled-up flyer in the mess around her. His heartrate went absolutely freaking crazy.

He bent, spoke soothing words to Trasher, reached for her shuddering body purposefully, pulled her from the dirt, then tenderly stroked her face as she shook and shrank, literally, from him.

"Listen to me, honey. I'll *never* hurt you. Sure, I'll make mistakes, but they'll be normal ones. Never ones that hurt you, or abuse you, and yes, you'll always know the difference. Honey." He held her arms as she stood before him, quivering. "Haven't we always treated you well? Listened to you?"

Her eyes widened, and for a minute he thought she was too far gone. Too many bad memories unleashed, remembered. The blood she talked about that one night in her sleep, the crusty cloak she wore around herself to ward off the pain—if everything hadn't been wrecked by Overbrand insinuating himself into her mind, into the fear that was still there, maybe she'd remember what Nate, Zach, and Og had meant to her.

This time Overbrand hadn't hurt an adult. He'd hurt this precious little being, this amazing creation. Rent her heart in two and collapsed the trust she'd finally given them.

That was the final straw.

In the distance, he heard someone take the microphone, announce the end of the successful show, and start thanking everyone for coming.

He was needed back there, should go, but in front of him was one very frightened little girl who meant more than all the accolades, all the show-closing speeches that needed to be made, for sales, positive cash flow, and good PR.

His heart constricted. What had she already gone through in her short life that she could be so quickly transported back to such a hateful world, to such fear and insecurity?

He had to make her strong. Let her know how wise she was. If he could do that… His gaze dipped again to the crumpled brochure.

"I think you're smart, honey. You're doing the right thing, even now. I'm not going to hurt you, but you have to make sure of it." He hated the way she shrank from him, but she was following natural instincts that had saved her more than once.

"I'm glad you're thinking, love. Always make sure you're safe. You've done that in the past, and your instincts were right."

He knew, intuitively, she was now back with him, by the slight change in her carriage. She'd left the dark place, even if only for a couple of moments. She was now here with him, in the barn. She'd made that part of the journey, already.

Though she was still unsure and not herself. Not her sweet, wild, unfettered self.

Inspiration hit him. "Don't forget. If you ever need anything from anyone, to feel safe—" anger bristled through him, thinking of anyone even trying to hurt their sweet, mouthy, wild little Trasher, "—you make sure you damn well speak up, okay? Don't ever hold back. If something doesn't feel right, speak up, and speak up loud, kid. Okay?"

A flicker in her eyes was his reward, though she stayed silent. However, the wheels were whirring in her mind. This kid was making calculations, decisions, like crazy.

One lone word popped out. "Even…" And she stopped.

He squeezed the thin arms where he held her, gently. One quick squeeze. Anything to get the blood pumping through her again. "Speak up, honey. Even …?"

The words spilled out, tumbling over themselves in their haste to be released before she thought better of it, before the fear constrained her, before the iron bands tightened around her once again. "Even with you?"

Yes. She was getting the point. Damn that Overbrand, but this conversation was still worthwhile, for the little girl he loved so much.

"Absolutely with me, honey. Especially with me, and with those who are closest to you. Always. With Og and Zachary, Galen too. Everyone. All of us at Hope House." He sighed, a bit of tension leaving his frame. "You're safe with us, and that means you can always speak up." His voice gentled. "Always say what's on your mind, no matter who you're with. Always and forever."

She watched him from under her brows. From under that mousy brown hair, the choppy, poorly cut, adorable chunks plastered around her face. "Okay."

Finally. Relief filtered through him. "Okay, sweetie." He heard the MC winding up for the finale, and could hear the question mark in his voice. Where's Nathan, damn him? He's supposed to be here.

They had to get back there. "Then let's…"

But her face abruptly crumpled, and her voice came out in a wail. "But Billy said really bad things. He said…"

Overbrand. Once again, spewing his vitriol. A dark anger came over Nathan. He knew what he had to do, no matter the consequences.

"This has gone far enough. I'm going to sort things out, honey, and put an end to all this, once and for all. Will you come with me? I'm going to talk in front of all those people, and tell them I really love you. To promise to always take care of you and treat you like a princess."

She blinked, and he saw the indecision in her eyes.

"If you want, I can ask Gram or one of the other ladies to come back and stay with you instead. But I'd love it if you'd come, hear me talk to everyone about this. About you, and us all, at Hope House. And how we treat each other." He held his hand out to her, waiting.

It felt like an eternity until she finally nodded and took his hand, the warmth from her little fingers the most welcome feeling in the world to him.

"Right then, come on, sweets. You and me, together, against the world. Let's go."

"Where have you two been?" Zach came at them as they emerged from the darkness. "I've been looking for you." His eyes widened at the change in Trasher's appearance. The torn dress, her unkempt hair with straw stuck in it, and the wet smears on her face.

He put his hand on her shoulder, squeezed, concern in his eyes, but with a quick shake of Nathan's head, he let it go.

"Good news, Nathan," he said hurriedly. "There's a top art reviewer here from New York, and he loves what he's seeing. I heard him say your show was fantastic, that there's never been anything like it. Especially in the gay world. This drivel," he nodded to a pile of flyers imprisoned in his grip, "almost ruined the show, but I think if we're careful, keep our heads about us, and don't call any attention to it, we can get through this without any damage. Don't feed the fire. I think you're going to get some good reviews, buddy. Possibly amazing ones. We may be able to fix up Hope House properly, make it a reality, and maybe..." His gaze slid to Trasher's. "Well, you know. If they let us. Finally."

Nathan purposefully transferred Trasher's hand to Zach's, curled his fingers around hers. He didn't answer him. "Don't let her go, no matter what."

A shadow passed over Zach's face. "What are you doing?"

"Make sure she's safe and doesn't run. Enlist Gram and Auntie."

"Nathan. What are you doing? Answer me."

He stared Zach straight in the eye, already light years away. "What I should have done years ago."

He strode toward the tiny platform they'd built from new pine, squeaky in its newness.

"Hey, folks." Jonas saw him approaching and smiled wide. He reached his arm toward him openly. "Looks like we're in for a special treat. Here's the star of the night. Nathan Gentael."

Nathan didn't smile. He ignored the hands stretched toward him, eager to shake his, as he forced his way through the crowd. He climbed up the two steps, made his way to the center, and stared out over the crowd.

There were more people than they'd thought would show. Way more.

He saw all the important people and his gut dipped at the recognition. If he chose to overlook the garbage that had been distributed tonight, if he played it low, right here, right now, it could possibly, potentially, blow over. His career could possibly start here, tonight. The big arc. The tail of the shooting star.

It was all here in his hands, if he wanted it. Once again.

If he played it safe. If he pushed down the accusations, let them disperse on their own. Not fan the flames. These prominent people, with decades in the business, had built reputations. They wouldn't want to get their hands dirty with this crap.

He scanned the crowd as everyone watched him, quiet, waiting for his opening words.

Then he caught sight of Trasher with Zach still clutching her hand. He remembered how she'd looked when they had left earlier for the show, how happy she'd been.

Now she looked like she'd lost her best friend—because she had. The lies had to be dealt with. He sucked in a deep breath, and jumped into the free fall, off the cliff.

"Friends. Welcome. I'm so honored all of you came. Some of you know me from years ago, but for many of you, I'm making your acquaintance for the first time tonight. Whichever camp you fall into, though, I'm thrilled that you trekked out to our rustic little spot to see some of my art."

He exhaled a sigh as silence fell around him. The bay breeze filtered in through the open barn doors a few feet away, curved down the path marked by the homespun barrels and golden chrysanthemums that Nellie, Courtney, Sandy, and all the rest of the Refuge Bay ladies had so carefully placed, and teased ocean scents through the crowd.

"But more, I'm glad you've come here to my home. To the beautiful community of Refuge Bay, where I got my start so many years ago." He knew what had to be done. What *he* had to do. "As you all know, I've been gone a while. Away from the art scene, and frankly away from life." He saw the brows furrowed, and quizzical looks came across many of the faces. "Why did I move away from everything I loved, everything that gave meaning to my life, and why did I distance myself from friends and family?" His voice lowered, thickened. "I'll tell you."

Suddenly, he didn't care. If this was the wrong thing to do from a PR standpoint, he'd deal. It was right from every other single point.

"Ten years ago, I let an enemy ruin my life. That enemy was potent, and strong. Not only did he ruin my life, but that of two of the people I care most about in the world—my mother and my father."

He swallowed roughly but pushed on.

"Because of the false accusations hurled against me, these two wonderful people lost their livelihood and their retirement savings. My father, an esteemed physician, lost his career. They lost their home, and they lost the love of the town they'd given their lives to in service. All because of false statements made by one vile man whom many people in this community decided to listen to. Shame on them for doing that to my parents. Shame on anyone who behaves that way to their neighbor."

Nathan looked around for Overbrand and didn't see him. The bastard was probably hiding like bullies do when they're called out.

"Today, they live in a tiny apartment in a town that doesn't know them. They live in isolation, and they tell me it's fine. They're good. They're happy, because they supported me and my art, the art you see all around you tonight. The richness has gone from their lives, and the toll is unforgiveable."

His insides were roiling, but he carried on.

"Back then, I did nothing. I was devastated, but I had a responsibility. Instead, I let this cruelty and its consequences curl me into a little ball and make me retreat from life in the hope no one would look at me or see me because I was ashamed. Not of my work or my life's course or my conduct, and certainly not of my art. I was ashamed because I couldn't fit into the tiny, narrow little box that horrible man and the people who believed him slotted me into."

A few people's eyes widened.

"Tonight, that horrible man has reared his ugly head again. There are accusations flying, saying that I've lived my life in self-interest, and not the interest of being good and kind, but a life fired with evil. Most atrocious of all, this hideous man had no problem undoing the life and happiness of a young girl. With lies and venom he's written that this young girl who came into my life and that of my best friend

Zach a short while ago is in danger in our care even though everything we have done has been legal and aboveboard, with the knowledge and participation of Child Protective Services. His hateful untruths were printed in pamphlets and well-placed statements made in receptive ears. What's been said and written has hurt the little girl we would do anything for. Who we consider our family."

Nathan looked at Trasher, who stood frozen beside Zach.

"Tonight, I confront that enemy. There is a man here tonight who has spewed lies and baseless accusations, but it is not that man I confront tonight, but other enemy who must be gone, forever, and that enemy is me."

The crowd gasped. Zach picked Trasher up and pulled her close against him.

"Five years ago, I allowed these rumors to splinter my life and that of my parents, and I ran. I hid, full of fear, thinking that what I'd given the world wasn't a gift, that it actually wasn't even a gift to me. That other people had the right to call the shots about my life. Instead of fighting, I hid."

He turned and spoke directly to Trasher.

"Let that be a lesson to you, sweet angel. If others call you out and say you have no right to be you, you throw it in their face and you walk proud because no matter what people say, you are a gift from the universe, and there's no one like you, nor will there ever be, sweetheart." His words thickened, and he choked, and suddenly all he saw was that little girl, and how her face eased.

"No matter who accused me, or came out against me, it was my job to stand up and claim my life. Be me, do me, and do it proudly. The past ends now and the future, the one I'm choosing, officially starts. Right here and right now."

Nathan scanned the gathering.

"Ladies and gentlemen, I am Nathan Gentael. I'm gay. The measure of a man, or of a human being is…" He paused a moment, took a deep breath. "I've been a coward in the past, and I regret it more than I can say. I've learned my lesson. My best friend is right over there, my aunt and gram are here. I love that little girl there like a daughter. The people I love, and Hope House, we're here to stay. If you don't like me, my art, my people, or what I intend to do with

Hope House, the door is over there by Bert Homestead, sitting in that old rickety chair. He'll gladly show you out.

"Know one last thing. The ground you stand on here tonight, that we all stand upon, is hallowed and sacred. This art and this event—living art of a kind—has been allowed to take place by the grace of my good friend, Sundance. Our lives are sacred, and we must live them in full recognition and truth of who we are, how we love, and what we create. Most of all, what we learn."

He took a quick glance at the sign beside him on the platform and laughed.

"When we created the title of this show, I had no idea how true it was going to be. Up until now, I would have run from it. But no more. Ladies and gentlemen, I am Nathan Gentael. Unwrapped."

He laid the microphone on the floor and left the platform.

Chapter Twenty-Eight

Og

Og hurried through the field to the barn. It was way past the show's closing. There were no cars in the area they'd roped off as a makeshift parking lot. The barn was dark, and there wasn't a light on in the ancient structure. The place was deserted, with nothing but the cool wind blowing past him.

Weird how a place that had felt like home only a few hours earlier could feel so different now. So lonely. When he left here, he'd been partner to the man he loved. Now he had no idea who he was.

He contemplated turning right around and heading for the house, but Nathan's show was in that old barn. The show he'd worked so hard to get him to put on, the show he'd hoped would burst him into the limelight.

With the twinkle in the two old ladies' eyes when art reviewers had been mentioned, he bet it had turned out spectacularly.

He had to go in and see for himself. A private showing, as it were.

Once inside the dark exterior, he found the master light switch, flicked it on, feeling like an intruder in the silence. The whole interior flooded with fairy lights. He gasped. The place, hewn with old wood and magnificent beams, all of that crisscrossed with tiny white lights, with the smell of earth and time around him, was magical.

The next thing that came to his mind was how much Trasher must've loved it. Felt the magic, the electricity. In her beautiful, fluffy, little girl's pink party dress. His princess. Even though he'd left her, left them all only a few scant hours earlier, and he had to bear that, his heart expanded.

Now his attention turned toward the subject matter. They'd talked earlier about curating the show in a specific manner. Having an area for people to talk and mill about in, and then another area, roped off and contained, for the erotic portion. Especially when Trasher was involved—no way were they going to keep her from the event. She was part of their family, at least for now, and she would be involved and welcome, so it was only appropriate to ensure that those areas were cordoned off.

He hadn't seen the final pieces Nathan had selected, or their placements. Only Nathan and Sundance knew that. Nathan had kept it a secret from everyone except the shrewd old man.

Og searched the illuminated barn. There was the small separate area off to one side, at the end of the exhibit, and the rest was open for everyone to see.

Focusing on the art, he couldn't help but feel stunned. Scenes of daily life in a rural community greeted him. More, the artist seemed to have picked moments of intense normalcy. Simple, but full of meaning. The eyes of a child as their father read them a bedtime story. Another kid's face, trusting and eager, when their mom put a bowl of spaghetti in front of them.

A mother holding her child close as it fell asleep, the love raw, yet gentle. In the moment, yet eternal. Not fleeting. Not temporary.

The more he saw, the more he realized Nathan had focused on moments of visceral love and great tenderness, the underlying message clear. Deep love was forever.

Og swallowed, allowing the tears to flow down his face as he took in more images. A man stopping to talk to an old-timer at the country store, one that looked like Cleotha's place, but wasn't. One of a thousand similar country stores dotted around the continent. The man, busy, the to-do list in his hand full of items, but his stance was relaxed and easy as if the old-timer was the most important thing in the world, his head tilted toward him, listening. The cell phone hanging from his pocket, most definitely off. The screen black.

Another image of a vivacious check-out girl in a small grocery store, encouraging one of the customers with what he imagined to be kind words, easing a lined, troubled forehead. The wonder in the customer's face showing as they thought of something else other than their troubles for a moment.

Throughout the exhibit, interspersed with and coupled with the larger paintings, were smaller canvases, studies of hands. The hands of the central characters in the main paintings, showing their interaction with others. At times tentative, at times giving a pat on another's hand. In one particularly moving one, an old hand covered a young person's, gripping it, transferring strength to it.

Og was floored. It was an absolutely stunning exhibition. Not only for the quality of the work, but more for its strong, yet simple and unbending message.

Love is all there is.

He'd fucked up. He'd lost this amazing man, and now he would never know the beauty of forever with him,

Finally, he walked to the cordoned section, and its tiny entrance.

Before a visitor entered, there was a study of two hands, as if two men were making love, one with his hands extended above his head, the other's gripping them tightly.

He stared at them, feeling like he'd been transported into another world, equally as alive to the one he was standing in right now. A mirror world.

With a jolt and a glance down at his own hand then back up again at the painting, he realized it was his hand. His bad hand, crooked in the way it gripped because of the injury he never spoke about. His hand and Nathan's. Entwined.

He looked down. Anything to take away the shock, the intensity of what he was feeling as it slammed through him. That's when he noticed it. There, in a tiny gap behind the concave wall-like structure, was another painting. He saw right away it was an alternate offering. Nathan must have considered replacing the painting now hanging, and then decided against it before going ahead with the one that was there now.

Them.

Holy god. With all he'd done to Nathan, with all his big talk of trying to make him stronger, the talk of protecting him forever, then abandoning him…Nathan was the stronger man. There was the proof of it.

He—they—were still the focus. The heart of the exhibition, you might say. With a tremor in his step, not knowing what any of it meant, he entered the enclosure.

They'd created a curved exhibit, a wall that was a big U, curving inward. One large picture in the middle, with smaller studies emanating from it. All being fed from the main image in the center. The pivotal image was erotic. Sexual.

With another hastily sucked in breath, he saw it was him and Nathan in the one erotic picture of the whole exhibit, when he'd thought it would be all erotic.

In the background, over the faint silhouette of a heart, barely discernible, they were making love. Og lost in the frenzy, the miracle of it. Nathan with his gaze open, watching every movement on Og's face. Og was lower, positioned more toward the bottom right-hand corner of the canvas.

Nathan had studied him. Knew every mood.

Hell. Og was the one unwrapped.

In that same bottom right corner, a gash. The slash through the painting.

The message stunning in its implication.

Imperfection was as strong a part of life as the good—and it was all perfect. Exactly as it was.

"Do you like it?"

Og jerked at the familiar voice, then sucked in a breath in an attempt to stop his heart from racing out of his chest. "I... I didn't know."

"That I know all your moods, that I catalogued you?"

Og was humbled. Utterly. "Yes. That."

Nathan skirted the exhibit, laid a finger on a smaller study, one that showed their knees touching under a table. Even though there was room on each of the chairs for them not to touch, they both sat on the respective edges of each chair, shimmied in as close together as possible so they could connect. Have contact.

"I'm an artist. I catalogue things."

Og shook his head. Pain, revelation, fear, and regret was a wicked stew boiling in his gut.

"Why did you leave?"

Shit. Fuck. "Palmer summoned me. I was told I had to leave you, leave Hope House, and be ready to move to another position. It was either obey or be gone. I didn't know what to do."

Nathan's mouth tightened, and he crouched to settle himself against the wall. "Money is important."

Og didn't care what happened next, he had to tell him.

"No. Not at all." He squatted in front of him, grabbed his hands. "Nathan. I wasn't supposed to tell you this, because it might put you in danger, but I can't hold it in any longer. Not when you think I care more about money than you."

Nathan pulled his hands free and averted his gaze.

"It's my brother. He was lost and stupid, and the people he was with turned on him. He's in a makeshift South American holding cell and I need to get him out. Alive."

Nathan's head snapped up in surprise. "What?"

"Michael. His name's Michael. We were abandoned young. It was only us. I failed him. I was older, figuring out my life, and didn't have time for him. He wanted my attention. He got into this gang and…."

Nathan's face was stony. "Is that why you divested all your possessions? Gave up your place? Stopped paying rent?"

Og nodded then shifted to sit on the floor beside Nathan, his back against the wall too. He hadn't realized Nathan had figured that out. Another surprise. Humbled again.

"I needed the money—still need it. The kid's in trouble." He heaved a heavy sigh. "I told Palmer to go to hell tonight. He said Hope House and my association with it is a liability for him. Either I leave you, or I left my job." Og shrugged. "I left my job. Now I've got do something about Michael, and fast…but," his voice tightened, and he had to push the words out with effort, "I had to come back. I couldn't leave you. I couldn't leave Trasher." He shook his head. "Even stupid Zach."

Nathan's face went dark. "Why didn't you tell me about this before? About your brother? We were partners, and you didn't share this with me."

The words were angry, full of pain, and he deserved it, but he had to get Nathan past that and back to *them*.

"My shit, not yours. I got myself into this mess with Michael. If I'd been a better parent… There were also threats that if I told anyone, they'd be next on the execution block." Og stared at the floor. "I'm not sure if that's true—they're small potatoes, but still unstable and cruel. I know enough about life to know unstable means bad things can happen at any moment, and you can't predict it. I couldn't take the chance, and even more so when the kid came along. I had to make sure you were all safe."

Nathan's gaze stayed narrow. "What are you going to do now?"

"I've burned my bridges with Palmer. I couldn't fulfill his conditions. Not if it took me away from you and Trasher."

Something in Nathan's face softened. "Under the circumstances, I'm not sure you did the right thing, but hell, I'm so glad you didn't run out on me."

Og's heart gave a sharp skip.

Stay honest. Now of all times, you have to stay honest. No matter the cost. "I did, for a few hours. We both know that. I can plead confusion, my brother's issues, the threat of losing him, but it killed me to be away from you. If you'll have me, Nathan Gentael, I'm here. Back. God knows I don't deserve you, but..." He swallowed, shaking, the unspoken plea coursing through his body.

Nathan...

His partner—not former partner, he prayed—gazed at a one-inch square on the opposite wall.

Og's heart was heavy. Fuck. It looked like he was done here.

His brain switched seamlessly to the other track. The other critical one. Even if he'd lost Nathan, there was no way he wasn't going to share what was in his heart anymore. It had to be an open damn book, even if Nathan didn't want to hear it. "But I have to get Michael out somehow. Get him safe. It's got to be my focus. The bastards have set a date to...." His voice cracked.

"To...?"

"Yeah."

Horror washed over Nathan's features. "I'll sell the house. You can have all the money. All of it. And if it's not enough—"

"No way I'm killing your dream. Your mission has to happen. If you can help me figure something out...."

"But—"

"No buts. You're going to have your dreams." In that moment, it dawned on Og that he didn't even know how the evening went.

"Nathan. How did the show go? Was it everything you hoped for? That we hoped for?"

For the first time, Nathan smiled. "Oh yeah, and more." As Nathan started relating the evening, a curious glow started in Og's chest. At least something had gone right. More than right. His man—for he would always be his, even if Nathan wouldn't take him back again—had come home again in so many ways.

Og's gaze lit on the central painting of the exhibit. The two of them locked in mutual passion, but more. There was energy running through the painting that said more than sex, more than a one-night stand.

Love.

He turned to Nathan. "It's been a long night. Maybe we could...could I stay?"

After everything he'd done that night, he didn't deserve to share the man's bed. Didn't deserve to feel the beating of his heart next to his, or the soft tenderness of Nathan's arm around his back as they spooned, one hand resting on Og's thigh.

He swallowed, unable to look at him anymore. Og had killed his chance at happiness.

Nathan reached forward and circled Og's hands with his smaller, more delicate artist's hands, and squeezed.

The moment expanded and filled the barn as time, life, and energy whirled around them.

When Og looked up into Nathan's warm gaze, Og knew they were good.

Nathan leaned forward and his lips met Og's. There was passion under the surface. More than passion though, the kiss was a welcome home. After five hours that had felt like five centuries, Og was back where he belonged.

Nathan broke the kiss, then his lips brushed Og's cheek in a tender caress. "Let's go home. I'm exhausted, and we've both been through the mill. I still don't know what the fallout is going to be, but I'll face it." He rose.

That phrase, *I'll face it,* taunted Og, reminding him of what he had inflicted on this gentle soul whom he loved with all his heart.

He reached up, grabbed his arm, making him stop before he turned. "Nathan. We'll face it. We'll face it together."

Nathan's expression filled a tiny chink in that big hole in Og's heart.

"My Atlas," Nathan murmured. "Let's go home."

***

Og

When they approached Hope House, nothing had ever looked so good. The old house in urgent need of repair, especially since the storm earlier that week had apparently knocked a casing loose, still looked like heaven. There was a light on in the kitchen, Zach left to guide them home by. Og was sure Trasher was safely ensconced in her bed.

An answering light glowed in the little cottage where their new tenant was now living. Galen was often up late into the night, and they wondered what kept him awake all those hours. That was his business, though a bit mysterious. Then he'd be up before dawn the next morning, working.

It was home, all of it. Og felt its odd protection as he walked in. However, he still couldn't shake the feeling that he was in a dream world. On the verge of joy, though not yet complete. Nathan's dream, as well as Og's absolute need to save his brother, all of it was still on hold, which was not a good place to be.

They creaked up the old stairs. They were in bed within a few minutes and fell into it gladly. They shared a soul-bending kiss, and their passion lit faster than Og could register fully.

Their ardor, not often demonstrated, was expressed with fierceness and beauty.

After, they fell asleep wrapped around each other.

Dark dreams haunted Og. It could all be over so fast, all of it, no matter how far they'd come.

In the morning, Og was woke by a rough jarring. "Seriously?" he muttered. "Nathan, for the love of god, quit—"

"It's not Nathan, it's me. Me-me-me-me-me-me-me. You guys gotta get up." Trasher was bouncing on their bed like a maniac.

He blinked. This was the little kid who'd been so upset last night? She sure wasn't unhappy now. What the hell? He pulled the sheet up over his bare chest. "Help."

"Breakfast's ready," she yelled, the words scrunched in between gasps for air. "Zach's calling it victory cakes and hash. Galen is there too, only he thinks the hash tastes like crap and won't tell Zach cause he liiiikes him."

"Okay, brat." Og shook the covers off himself, and yes. He was wearing pajama bottoms. "Get your face washed, your hair combed, and we'll meet you downstairs for breakfast. Go."

"Hair combed?" Trasher repeated with disgust. "Since when?"

"Since you're learning to be a lady. You know, one of those people who wears those gorgeous pink dresses?"

Trasher's face fell, and she stopped talking.

Oops. That was a mistake.

"You know that other pink dress you liked at the shop? The one you wanted more than the one we ended up buying, cause their stock was low?"

She raised her eyes to his, and her brow furrowed. "Yeah."

"I seem to remember it was coming in your size."

Her eyes widened as if her eyelids were pulled upward by a string. "Really? We get to buy that one?"

"Almost anything can be done in life, honey. Remember that." He swatted her on her pajama-clad butt. "If you comb your hair."

"Hell, I'll wash my face for that, too." Og winced at the curse word, but he was learning. One, or at the most ten, battles at a time with this kid. He'd talk to her later. She leapt from the bed, skidded on the throw rug, bringing on another wince, and ran from the room.

When he turned back to Nathan, he was met with a querying look. Nathan's gaze focused on his face, then dipped to his PJs.

"I put these on after…when I went to the bathroom."

"And they stayed on because…"

"Because a little girl lives in the house, and you never know when you might need to tend to her."

"Or find her bouncing on your bed in the morning. Hey, do you think we've scarred her for life?"

Og snorted. "Love and stability don't scar. Abusive foster parents are the devil and I can't tell you what I'd like to do to them."

Nathan grabbed his hand and squeezed, a serious look on his face. "Ditto." He sighed. "Now let's go down and face the fallout."

Chapter Twenty-Nine

Nathan

"The homecoming warriors." Zach waved a spatula in the air while standing in front of the stove finishing the last of the pancakes. "Come and get it."

Nathan smiled and tried to put on the best show he could for his friend and the little girl he'd wanted so desperately to make part of his family. He still couldn't suppress the big ball that was forming in his throat.

After that crazy show last night—he still wasn't sure how that was going to go, but he surmised it couldn't be good—something more important was happening today.

Mrs. Merriwether had called yesterday and told him she'd be there at noon to pick up Trasher. They'd found a foster home, and it was time for the child to be relocated. The little elf who had been occupying their lives was almost out the door, and he didn't know how he'd stand it, or how he'd help her get through it. At the moment, she seemed to be riding some type of false high. No doubt she'd fall soon, and he'd have to be there for her, no matter how he was feeling.

Damn it. Why did she have to leave?

Og had been cheerful, but Nate had seen the black cloud in those deep green eyes when he thought Nathan wasn't looking. With his brother in trouble and no money to continue the rescue efforts, it was a desperate situation. It bothered Nathan so badly that when he'd gone to the bathroom for a drink of water in the middle of the night and had bumped into Zach, they'd sat and talked, and Nate had told him everything.

He hoped Og was okay with him telling Zach, but Og's problems were now all of theirs, and the big guy would have to get used to that.

"Here, here, here." Trasher grabbed the back of the chair beside her. "Here."

Galen, at the counter with Zach for a change, smiled at her. "Give them a second, boo. Let them wake up."

It seemed Trasher was growing on him too, especially with the time he was finally starting to spend in their company. The man was turning up a fair bit lately, especially around a certain person.

"Who put firecracker powder in your OJ this morning?" Og snarked.

Her response was an impish grin and a glance at Zach, who was carrying the steaming frying pan to the table. "Now?"

"After breakfast." Zach tossed a glance at the paper. "Someone ran out and got you two ogres a bunch of art magazines this morning."

Nathan ogled it, surprised to see the banner. "To New York?"

"Now, dear, really?" Aunt Tilley remonstrated as she ambled into the kitchen from what used to be Zach's room, which she'd taken over without apology. "He was up at four-thirty this morning, left the peninsula, and went to see Frank Szabo, one of my contacts from my Big Apple days. I pressed him with the task of getting us all the reviews on Unwrapped." She sniffed the air with a modicum of distaste. "He may not know how to cook a flapjack, but the man certainly is loyal, and knows how to follow direction."

Zach shimmied a thin cake off the fry pan onto the Darth plate. "Pancake. Not flapjack. Part of the reason I did all that is because a certain someone came to my door at four in the morning, banged like a banshee out of freakin' hell, and suggested I do it."

"Well, well, dear, don't go on about that now. How was I to know that you and our new tenant were—"

They all did a double take, except for Trasher. They stared at Zach, then Galen, both of whom turned red.

Leave it to Aunt Tilley to show up at the right moment.

"Galen, you're red." Trasher stated the obvious. Then she turned to Nathan. "Galen stopped someone from breaking into the house last night. He said they came thinking we'd all be gone. Galen ran him off. Got in a couple of good ones too, I bet."

"He did? Why didn't I hear about this?"

Galen looked away. "Not a big deal, man. You guys were gone. Up to me to protect the place. I did. End of story."

"You're holding Nathan up," Gram chided as she came in through the back door. "For crap's sake, let him read the reviews. We've all had a go. Wait," she interrupted herself. "Just wait. Here she comes."

A white and tan blur streaked past her, headed for Trasher, then segued to Zach and the frying pan.

"Molly," Trasher screeched.

The excited dog leapt onto Zach with both paws, and in an attempt to save the breakfast and also not hurt the dog, the frying pan traveled in a huge arc as he swiveled. It barely missed Nate and, in a move defying the laws of physics, was caught by Galen's oven-mitted hands.

"Whoa," Trasher yelled. "That's chill."

Apparently another *fait accompli* by the man who was starting to prove himself indispensable around the place. Interesting, Nathan mused.

Most importantly, the pancakes made it to the table, joined the waiting hash and bacon, and the ever-present mound of animal cookies. Molly deposited her furry behind on the checkered tile, hoping for a reward or a handout.

With the ebb of activity, everyone's gaze turned to Nathan.

He fell into the chair beside Trasher and raised the first paper from the pile with a shaking hand and no breath in his lungs.

His eyes lit on the paper and his world flipped upside down.

Gentael is *back*.

The first line of the article said: "Thank god."

"Here's another one." Trasher unceremoniously dropped the next paper on top of the one he was reading, having ensured the edges were well coated with jam. "Read that one, too."

The wacky little art show in the barn on the peninsula births a not-to-be-missed event for all men. For All People. Don't miss it.

They kept coming. Largely positive, some glowing.

He closed his eyes and let himself feel the immensity of it all. It had been so damn long.

He knew who he had to thank for it. There was only one man who'd been able to cajole, coax, and damn well forced him to hold that art show.

Jake Augustine "Boom Boom" Reiden. The boxer from New York.

He reached over to touch Og's hand. Nate couldn't say everything that was pulsing in him, but if could say it with a touch, he would.

The answering look Og gave him about melted his heart.

I'm here for you. Always.

Og rose. Ever since last night, since Nate had learned about Michael, Nate swore he saw Og thinking about his brother and the situation all the time. Like now.

"I gotta get out."

"You want me to come?"

Og shook his head. "No. Just need a few."

He disappeared out the back door.

"You happy, hon?" Grams laid a hand on Nathan's forearm, bringing his mind back into the kitchen. "We're so proud of you. Your mom and dad, too. They're sending more reviews along. They're over the moon."

"I can't believe this, to be honest. Especially with Overbrand and all his lies."

"After what you did?" Zach sat at the table with them. "I heard from that Frank guy that he thinks Overbrand's future is in question. His employers aren't any too happy. He may have to resign himself to puff pieces for the *National Spyer* from now on. He's suited for that work, for sure."

"Overbrand slapped down. That I can live with."

"So, if everything is good..." Gram balanced a mountain of jam on a tiny teaspoon en route to her stack of flapjacks. "What's eating you?"

Nathan couldn't hold it in any longer. "Og's got a few serious family issues."

Gram snorted. "Who doesn't?" She slapped the jam on the pancake, then went back to the bottle for the second mountain. "More to the point, what can we do to drop-kick whoever's hurting the man?" She nodded at them. "Do not discount the kick in an old lady who has nothing to lose."

What a weird little family they had.

Trasher kept throwing Zach furtive little glances. What the hell was going on?

Nate noticed with pleasure that her plate was stacked. Her *Cinderella* plate. Yes, she had both in front of her. Darth and Cinderella, but Cinderella was winning this morning.

Progress.

He wasn't sure if that princess dress had helped, but if she was his child, his and Og's, they'd dump so much princess crap on her, she'd choke.

If only.

"Anything to help Og is a go." Aunt Tilley raised her thumb. "If we could float a bit of civil disobedience into it, all the better."

"Can I go to Jonas's place later?" Trasher was still bouncing in her chair like somebody had wound her up and she was never going to come down. Nathan's heart cramped again. Another couple of hours. But he had to help her through the transition, much as he loved seeing her this happy.

He cleared his throat. "Listen, I don't want to rain on anybody's parade, but we've all got to face it. Honey, are you packed yet? You know Ms. Merriwether's coming for you at noon."

Suddenly, everyone was beaming at him. Zach, Gram, Tilley, and, most of all, Trasher.

"What is going *on*? Will somebody tell me, please?"

Trasher got out of the old wooden chair and slowly leaned into him, gave him a big hug, her cheek against his chest. "I'm not going anywhere."

"Wha—" He pushed her away, holding her at arm's length. "We talked to them about making you our little girl, honey, but they said no. You can't hide out here, much as we all want that. We have to keep your life legal. It's for the best." He felt the tears welling in his eyes at the little girl who was trying to find any way to stay with them.

"Um, she's right, Nathan." Zach looked at him, and he noted the sheen in his eyes too. "A Miss Braden called early today. You know her?"

"April Braden? Hell yeah. She knew me when I was in school. We were in college at the same time, too. She works at CPS, but she isn't on Trasher's case."

"Well, she got switched. Something about helping out an old friend."

"What?"

"I took matters into my own hands," Zach explained. "I talked to a few people and found this April you'd spoken about a few times. I had a conversation with her. The other parents didn't fall through. It was more that when April talked to Trasher—we didn't want to tell you because you were so loaded down preparing for the show—and investigated you and Og and me too, she felt there weren't any better parents on earth for this little Emily imposter."

Trasher unceremoniously batted him with a swipe of her jam-laced palm.

Right at that moment, Og opened the back door and came in, his hand curled around his cell phone.

Zach caught Trasher's hand in mid-air, squeezed it, and scooped her onto his lap. "There are a few legalities yet to take care of, but this little one is ours. Og, you missed it. CPS reconsidered. Trasher's ours. Actually yours. Yours and Nathan's. If you'll have her."

By the abrupt jolt that visibly went through the man, and the look in Og's eyes, she was already his. "Dear god," he murmured. "Thank you."

Suddenly, Trasher started bouncing crazily on Zach's lap. She yelled, even as he winced. "I never have to go away, ever again. Ever-ever-ever-ever-ever."

Nathan stole a quick glance at Og. The man's face was transformed, but it wasn't only the news about Trasher. There was something else.

He put his balled-up fist on his chest and held it there. "Now what?"

The whole kitchen fell silent. For once, the two old ladies stopped nattering. Everyone was looking at Og.

"I had a conversation with Palmer and…I'm back. Reemployed. Full salary, well, actually a bump up, plus benefits. Which I'm exchanging the value of—for the short-term—for more cash. For you know what."

"Michael," Trasher yelled once more, bouncing higher on Zach's lap.

Og stared at her, eyes wide. "How do you know about—"

Zach hugged Trasher close. "That's our little secret, honey."

Nathan couldn't believe what he was hearing. The whole morning had been surreal. He wasn't used to this much good news. "Explain."

Og crossed to him, took his hands, and Nathan felt them shaking. "Because of you."

Nathan blinked. "Me?"

"Palmer wanted to know how your show stacked up—I'd told him about it last night—and Hope House. When he read what you did at the end—in a major newspaper—he changed his mind. He said Hope House was exactly the kind of charity he wanted to be connected with."

"You serious?"

"He also said that any man who can do what you did was a man to be admired and to be trusted."

It was really too much. The joy, the feeling that he'd come full circle, only to a better place than he'd started out in. No matter what anyone said, he knew, it was all thanks to the man standing in front of him.

And Zach.

And the little girl who'd pushed him to be who he really was.

Plus, his Gram, Aunt Tilley, and his parents.

Even Molly sitting there, wagging her tail because she could.

His family.

Holding tight to Og's hand, he dropped to his knees in front of Trasher. He held out his arms, and she flew into them, Galen watching with a grin. Og joined him, and soon they were all hugging the little girl, even Molly getting joyous barks in, licking wherever she could get a swipe in, her cold black nose darting everywhere as she whined happily.

Nathan hugged Trasher hard, laid his lips against her cheek, and whispered to her. Joy arced in him when he realized she was hugging him for the first time with her fists uncurled. Her open hands laid on his back, pressing into him.

The balled-up little fists, protecting herself, were gone.

He had to ask her. Hear it from her own mouth. "Do you want to stay with us, Trasher, princess or Emily, whoever you decide you'll be today? Are you okay with this, honey?"

"I have two dads. Animal cookies. I've got a crazy uncle who makes quiche, my gram, Aunt Tilley, and Molly." She gasped, sucked in one huge breath and uttered her final decree. "I'm home, forever. Hell. I'm absolutely bitchin'."

Epilogue

Nathan

The Mustang's door was ajar. Zach, Nathan, and Trasher were piled in. The glorious warm breeze of a summer morning in its heyday wafted around them. Teal-blue waves rolled and crashed a short distance away, providing the bounty that everyone on the tiny peninsula lived for. Tourists would soon be coming, finding the beauty in the area irresistible.

Today was serene and joyous. Reserved only for those fortunate enough to be living on Refuge Bay.

Trasher jumped furiously in the car, making it rock. "Princess," Nathan snapped. "Stop it. You don't want to wreck the springs of Og's baby, now do you?"

"Not princess today. Darth," she yelled, but stopped her wild jumping. "It's not only Og's car. It's yours, too." She donned a beatific expression. "What's mine is yours and yours is mine."

"Og. What the heck's keeping you?" Zach reached over and pumped the horn. "Get a move on. We'll be late. Jonas and FireStar won't wait forever."

"He's gotta wait," Trasher wailed. "I gotta ride SkyLark. FireStar, too. After Gemma. I got to."

"Hush, child. I'm only trying to get him to hurry. They'll wait. All of Refuge Bay will be there for the picnic and potluck at Briarhedge. Galen, Gram, and Tilley will watch out for your interests, don't worry. Jonas won't let anyone else ride your stallion until you get there."

"But Galen's there," Trasher yelled, pointing. Indeed, the handsome bearded man came around the back of the cottage, a suitcase in hand. Not where they'd expected him to be.

"What?" A surprised sound escaped Zach at the sight of the suitcase. "Is that old garbage he's cleaning up still?"

"I heard him saying good-bye to Molly this morning, and that he's packing." Trasher, suddenly upset, sat. "I don't want him to go. He said he was leaving, and he'd never forget her. I don't want him to go. Daddy, can you tell him to stay?"

This was new info, and not pleasant, especially to the man in the backseat. "I'll talk to him tonight. I'll find out what's going on. And—"

His phone cut him off as it vibrated. Palmer.

The man had been after them both lately, him and Og, to come and inspect Hope House himself. *Why a man with his money and his clout wants to come and spend time with us, I'll never know. He's used to the finest five-star hotels and instead he wants to spend a day with us?*

Og had reassured Nathan it was merely a due diligence thing, before he backed Hope House with more funds. Nathan would be fine playing host for a walk-through, no worries. Especially if it meant additional funding.

He listened to the message, nodding to himself distractedly. He made a mental note: *Deal with this later tonight, too.*

Right now was about family. Their little family, and the bigger family of Refuge Bay, all getting together for a huge, communal potluck. He mentally shelved all the new issues popping up, and not a moment too soon.

The back door slammed, and Og strode toward them.

"Dad." They all stared at him. The expression on his face. "What?"

He strode directly toward Trasher. Scooped her out of the seat, twirled with her, her expression surprised, amid yelps of *we'll be late* mutating to shrieks of joy. "They called, sweetheart. Paperwork's final. You're not going anywhere. You're staying with us."

They stopped, stood against the breeze that fluttered her cotton blouse, and his khaki pants. "For reals?"

"For reals." He pressed lips to her cheek, gave her a resounding smack, but his eyes were shuttered.

That man, Nathan thought, heart so big, underneath all that steel casing, which was getting thinner every day. It would probably always be there. The man was tough, would always protect those he loved.

As would Nate and Zach.

The men of Hope House. The start of something special.

With Og finally in the driver's seat and Trasher with Zach in the back, the 'Stang rumbled to life. Nathan's hand snaked toward Og's, grasping it tightly. "Any news yet?"

"Watcher told me they're in position. They'll pick the right time. Could be today. They're on it."

"I'm here for you. We all are."

An answering squeeze, long and hard.

"Can we go? Please, Dad?"

Nathan's heart jumped again. Og was Dad. Nate was Daddy. Zach was Zach, or Unc Z. A perfect solution, and she'd come up with it herself. Their little girl.

"Yes, wiggle-wart. We can." Og gunned the gas, then turned and flashed Trasher a quick smile and winked at Zach and Nathan. "FireStar will never know what hit him."

He trained his gaze straight ahead as the car started to gain traction as they headed to their day of fun and toward their future. Together.

"Okay, y'all. Hang on to your hats. Weeeee's a rumblin'."

ABOUT THE AUTHOR

Susan loves romance, and believes it's a staple ingredient to life. She uses this to create sexy, heart-warming romances where friendship and passion, plus a certain amount of risk intertwine to create a love that is timeless.

Cheerfully addicted to homemade green smoothies (and the rewarding prospect of grossing out certain close friends who shall remain nameless), she also plays second fiddle to the feline masters in her life.

CONNECT WITH SUSAN:
website: susansaxx.com
twitter: @susansaxx
instagram: @susansaxxbooks
facebook: SusanSaxxAuthor
linkedin: susan-saxx-44953b46

www.BOROUGHSPUBLISHINGGROUP.com

If you enjoyed this book, please write a review. Our authors appreciate the feedback, and it helps future readers find books they love. We welcome your comments and invite you to send them to info@boroughspublishinggroup.com. Follow us on Facebook, Twitter and Instagram, and be sure to sign up for our newsletter for surprises and new releases from your favorite authors.

Are you an aspiring writer? Check out www.boroughspublishinggroup.com/submit and see if we can help you make your dreams come true.

www.ingramcontent.com/pod-product-compliance
Lightning Source LLC
Chambersburg PA
CBHW031340170626
46807CB00002B/774